THE BRUMBACK LIBRARY
OF VAN WERT COUNTY
VAN WERT, OHIO

THERE'S A
CUPID IN
MY SOUP

THERE'S A
CUPID IN
MY SOUP

•

GAIL HAMILTON

AVALON BOOKS
THOMAS BOUREGY AND COMPANY, INC.
401 LAFAYETTE STREET
NEW YORK, NEW YORK 10003

PRINTED IN THE UNITED STATES OF AMERICA
ON ACID-FREE PAPER
BY HADDON CRAFTSMEN, SCRANTON, PENNSYLVANIA

THERE'S A
CUPID IN
MY SOUP

Chapter One

"Pick him up at one, drop him here at four to meet the brass. Meantime, tour him round our fair city and chat him up nicely, Sophie. There's a dear."

Greer Delaney, sometime anchor of CAM TV News, was already on the run, the light of pursuit in her eye as well as delight at having escaped another of the boring PR duties her high profile thrust upon her. Sophie Moore, Greer's much-burdened assistant, halted mid-stride as her boss flung out of the newsroom, off to the story that had broken only minutes before. A story so big even Greer needed to report from the scene.

"Who?" Sophie called, charging down the hall after Greer and the camera crew. Then, realizing that Greer was once again going to abandon her on the sidelines, she clutched Greer's crisp linen sleeve. "Oh Greer, you promised, you *swore* I could go along the next time something spectacular broke. . . ."

Though as yet only a lowly research assistant, Sophie's heart burned to be on the news trail with Greer and the others. In the six months she had been at CAM she had tried every conceivable ploy to get out of the station and into the heart of the action.

Greer paused in flight, flashing the famous smile that beamed across Toronto evenings at six. She had a good seven inches on Sophie and was so rakingly elegant she looked able to slice steel with her profile. She was also wise to her assistant.

"Nice try, dear, but you should know by now to get dread oaths down in writing. I need you charming the argyles off one Claude Lacomte. He's the Buckeroo's new golden boy, so I'm counting on you to make him happy. And," Greer added gleefully, "convey my heartfelt regrets at not greeting him myself."

The Buckeroo was what everyone called Jock Owen, station manager and majority stockholder. A hard-bitten survivor from the heyday of print, Jock had parted ways with a dozen radio stations before settling his maverick self to run the small, but certainly scrappy, independent television station. His cowboy tactics were both the admiration and the despair of his own staff and of his arch competitor, CXRT, on the other side of town. Toronto audiences tuned in with relish to the ongoing dogfight between the two pugnacious rivals.

Greer took off again. Sophie galloped doggedly behind.

"Who's Claude Lacomte?"

"That new celebrity chef Jock's hired. Don't take him to any hamburger joints along the way!"

Greer vanished, leaving Sophie in the corridor, the blood of a born journalist pumping through her veins and the slam of steel doors echoing in her ears. She turned back with a sigh. A cook! The rest were off chasing what might be the biggest insurance scam of the decade and she was stuck baby-sitting a cook!

Drawing three deep breaths, Sophie vowed to be pleasant to the unknown Claude despite her homicidal thoughts. If she were to succeed in the news business, cool-eyed objectivity must prevail over her own impulsive, unfortunately headlong nature. After all, it was not for nothing that Sophie had come out tops in the fierce competition for one of the few entry-level jobs at CAM. If she had to put in her time as a drudging gofer, then she'd be the best drudging gofer the station had ever seen. Greer Delaney was the most respected newswoman in the city. Sophie meant to follow in Greer's footsteps no matter how arduous the trail. Then, someday, she too would speak weighty words into the camera's unwinking stare while a whole nation—well, a bit of the nation, at least—would sit up smartly and listen! The never failing stars returned to Sophie's eyes as she hurried down the hall. She had barely half an hour to get herself to her rendezvous with Claude Lacomte.

"Look out!"

Jimmy "The Bean" Cort, who manned the sports desk, sprang to save his files from Sophie's elbow. Sophie tucked her arm in hastily and tossed a rueful grin.

"Sorry."

Jimmy nodded, following Sophie's energetic form wistfully. Like the rest of the newsroom staff, he'd learned to be alert when Sophie was around. Sophie lived her life as a speeding human dynamo and, as such, was a flying menace to loose papers, free-standing coffee cups, upright briefcases, and empty chairs. Oddly, few people grew angry when they fell victim to Sophie's enthusiasm, for how could anybody complain about someone whose mind was so obviously on greater things? Besides, Sophie always apologized profusely when something crashed to the floor. Profusely, sincerely, and with a smile that would melt the heart of Scrooge himself. The harder she tried to be careful, the more mugs toppled to their doom. For a serious, ambitious person such as Sophie, clumsiness was but a minor inconvenience in her grand-scale scheme of life.

"Where are you off to so fast?"

Agnes Reardon, who was not only the newswriter but Sophie's roommate and dearest childhood friend, looked up from her keyboard. She kept her coffee cup under her printer, out of Sophie's range.

"PR job. Got to pick up somebody named Claude Lacomte and give him the quick and easy sight-seeing tour before he meets the Buckeroo. Greer was supposed to do it but she's off behind the fire trucks like everyone else."

Sophie sighed again and gazed at the door through which Greer had departed. Agnes, who, in contrast to Sophie's compact figure, was tall and thin with the face of an apprentice wise woman, furrowed her brow.

"Claude . . . ? Oh that Claude! Wow! He's fresh from a gold medal in the Culinary Olympics. And quite a dish himself if rumor speaks the truth."

Agnes chortled at her own pun while Sophie leaned to retrieve her coat from the rack.

"Culinary Olympics? Surely you jest."

Agnes shook her head. "Uh-uh! I kid you not. It's a serious, world-class event. Each country enters a team. With captains and everything. Claude was Canada's captain. He brought home the gold—or should I say the bacon!"

The coatrack rebounded off the wall, swayed on its three metal feet, and regained its composure. Sophie searched for her sleeve opening, not knowing whether to believe Agnes or not. Besides torturing the entire building with her puns, Agnes was capable of the most outrageously plausible put-on. How she ever got entrusted with hard news copy, Sophie never knew.

"Honest," Agnes repeated. "He's to be the new shining light of afternoon TV. The Buckeroo's brainchild, hired at great expense to scintillate on the new gourmet show. Ladies will swoon into their *sauce hollandaise* and the ratings will drag us above the bankruptcy line. Enjoy!"

"A cooking show!" Sophie cried incredulously. "CAM has never run a cooking show. Besides, there aren't any ladies home cooking in the afternoon anymore."

"The Buckeroo doesn't know that. And none of us mice down here are going to spring the awful news."

Sophie shrugged into her trench coat, the first necessary purchase of any would-be newsperson, and hunted for her purse.

"Of course," Agnes added, plucking a strand of pale hair from her eyes, "the Buckeroo is also gambling on yuppie burnout and a horde of panicked baby boomers stuck home with babies produced seconds before their biological clocks conked out. The old fox might be wilier than we imagine."

That was the ongoing debate at CAM—whether the boss

was smarter than the lot of them put together, or just plain crazy. Opinion remained forever divided as the station bucked financial adversity year after year, listing, careening, and wallowing, but never quite going under. Sophie shook her head.

"I thought cooking shows went out with the fifties. Who even cooks their own food in this day and age?"

"Certainly not you," Agnes laughed, referring to Sophie's complete disinterest in food except as fuel shoveled indiscriminately in whenever the old energy level started to dip. The closest Sophie came to having a food preference was her addiction to Galaxy Cakes, gooey chocolate and cream concoctions bought off the snack shelves in individual packages and injected with enough preservatives to keep them fresh into the twenty-second century. Agnes herself was a vegetarian who seemed to live on air and carrot sticks. Between the two, the tiny kitchen of their shared flat resembled an abandoned storage closet full of stacks of paper, scattered teacups, and Sophie's collection of *Teach Yourself* Russian and Arabic phrase books.

"Besides," Agnes observed as Sophie headed for the door, "you can be sure Jock didn't hire this Claude for his recipes. There's only one way a show host makes it these days—and that's on twenty-four-karat sex appeal!"

Sex appeal! Sophie hooted and gurgled all the way to the parking lot, and her faithful clunker. The only images her mind threw up were Uncle Ben, Mr. Chips, and her three childhood favorites, Snap, Crackle, and Pop. Oh, and she mustn't forget the Pillsbury Doughboy or the Jolly Green Giant. The Green Giant wasn't too bad—if you liked your men the size of skyscrapers and the color of broccoli.

More pertinent matters soon took over Sophie's mind. All the way to the hotel where she was to meet her charge, her attention dwelt on the blazing construction site Greer was even now arriving at. Tonight's lead story for sure. Greer would stand dramatically outlined against billowing flames and smoke-stained firemen. Sophie wondered how many minutes Mavis, the news director, would allot and filed away her guess to check against the actual timing. Technical details, lead-ins, punchy, pithy, no-holds-barred commentary unrolled in Sophie's imagination. Her gut tugged to drive straight to the scene and let Claude the chef go to Hades. If she were there, she might spot one angle, see, overhear something the others had missed. And if she were ever to get in front of a camera, with a microphone in her hand . . .

Sophie's heart thudded faster at the thought. The pinnacle of her ambition, the desire of her bosom, was to be deep in the fray, hard-driving, ruthlessly observant, ferreting out the truth no matter how carefully buried. Oh yes, no matter how hard she had to work, she'd get on the CAM news crew. And after CAM there'd be a bigger station, then a network. She'd put in her time as a foreign correspondent, plunging fearlessly into the cauldrons where history forged. . . .

A lurch, accompanied by a gritty crunch, jerked Sophie out of her dream. Rats! She was already in the hotel parking lot, her bumper buried in the fender of a very low, very red, very expensive Porsche. The doorman appeared as though conjured from smoke, palm clapped to forehead.

"Not that one! Oh, there's going to be the devil to pay!"

Before Sophie could get a word out, the man was gone again. With a practiced eye, Sophie inspected the damage and started to write down the car's license number. A Quebec plate, she noted. Probably a tourist. A rich tourist, she amended, whom she hoped was of the good-natured variety. She barely had the last digit down before the doorman was bearing down on her again, followed by a rangy, fluidly moving man who had the rather dangerous look of a wolfhound loping to the hunt. Sophie knew at once he was the owner of the car—for only such a man could own such a car. And owners of such cars were apt to become unhinged at the sight of the faintest little scratch.

"It's not serious," Sophie informed him soothingly, long experience having taught her that the best defense was a good, calm offense. A car's purpose, Sophie believed, was

to get one from A to B in the most efficient possible time—
or the fastest—depending on the story to be covered. Obstacles en route were incidental, as the many dents and
scrapes ornamenting Sophie's own vehicle attested. What
were a few bangs when it ran like a top and the agility of
its brakes and steering saved her regularly from larger disaster? "The best body shop for foreign cars is down on
King Street. Luigi'll have this ironed out in a jiffy."

Sophie braced herself. To her surprise, the fellow didn't
shout, rage, or throw hysterics. Sophie had seen all three—
and from the most unexpected people. Instead, he stalked
silently around both vehicles, inspecting the damage, his
hands tucked into his pockets, lips pressed firmly together
over whatever expletives welled inside. As he moved,
Sophie examined him closely, for a good reporter must be
able to size up anyone in the space of a few swift seconds.
Her usually acute mental processes had only one thing to
say:

Sexy! In bright neon letters with glitter on top!

Sophie stifled the start of a grin. Chalk one up for Agnes!

Nevertheless, the description fit. Even Sophie, who ran
on her intellect all day, ignoring such indefinables as physical attraction, had to admit it. From the shock of amber
hair loose on the man's forehead, to the lean, prowling
grace of his walk and the emphatic bones of his face, the
fellow emitted maleness insistent as a drumbeat. More than
that, he had a powerful hint of intensity about him that
hummed in rhythm with Sophie's own inner drive.

So stop staring!

Good reporters remained neutral and Sophie wasn't too
good at that part yet. Shifting gears, she sped on with her
analysis.

Organized, she guessed. Affluent. Not a man to cross
unnecessarily. And, from the decisiveness of his movements, used to getting his own way. He also liked clothes.
Only a man who liked clothes would be wearing that wine-
striped shirt, that handwoven tie clipped in with gold and
those knife-creased gray trousers so understated they could

only be of the finest Italian wool. And only such a man would encase all this splendor in a to-die-for leather jacket so soft and supple, so subtly styled and textured that Sophie's very fingers cried out to bury themselves deep in its buttery folds.

Sophie balled her hands into fists. Though she lamented her own questionable fashion sense, she knew expense when she saw it. She had researched all the pricey designers in order to spot public servants and overactive evangelists spending more than their up-front salaries seemed to warrant.

Caressingly, the fellow ran his hand along the Porsche's fender right down to where Sophie's bumper jammed it in against the tire. Sophie's attention whipped back to his body. Wide shoulders, flat stomach, lots of hard wiry muscles to carry the clothes so well. No squishy paunch crept over this beltline. The man must spend half his week in the gym. Or be an international tennis competitor. Athlete seemed to be written all over him, yet was contradicted by that cool air of command. A big-time business exec, Sophie speculated. Or perhaps an airline pilot out in his civies. Yet could even a captain afford the wardrobe this fellow carried on his back?

Ah-ha! Sophie caught the flush working up the fellow's jawline. Temper did reside in that resilient body. A volatile temper, no doubt, given to delayed but spectacular explosion. Perhaps that was why the doorman had taken up a defensive position behind the lamppost. Sophie snatched the initiative.

"You're parked on the yellow stripes," she pointed out. "It says 'No Parking' underneath your left rear wheel."

"Were you competing for the same spot, or did you mean to take a stab at the driveway?"

The asperity of tone could have scraped the paint off the fender all by itself, but Sophie had no intention of getting angry. If she did, he'd have her on the run. Besides, a jab or two was fair enough when the injured party had left a parked car in one piece and returned to find it squashed in by a perfect stranger in a trench coat. She had turned too tightly on the narrow bend.

"Actually, I was aiming for that empty space over there. I'm supposed to pick up a guest from the lobby."

She turned on her high-beam smile, just to show the event was too trivial to waste breath over. Guilelessly, she looked into his eyes—which turned out to be so startlingly green she forgot to track the progress of the flush on the rest of his face. It deepened suddenly, then faded, as though by effort of will. From an inside pocket he produced a small notebook bound in calfskin and accompanied, naturally, by a slim gold pen.

"I assume you have insurance," he said in a voice that implied the insurance companies had abandoned her years ago.

"Of course." Sophie accepted philosophically that car insurance was going to be one of the major expenses in her life.

They exchanged information, Sophie writing everything down in her tumbling script. As the man began to tuck his pen away, Sophie, veteran at this, stopped him.

"You've forgotten something."

"What?"

"Your name."

She couldn't help looking at his eyes again, still the most disconcerting thing about him. Leaf-colored eyes, alive with interest in everything around him. Eyes that hinted they could look through you if they wished. Eyes tilted slightly, thickly lashed. Curiosity lived in them, and challenge. Yet, noting the laugh lines too, Sophie relaxed a trifle. A man with humor in him was not so likely to demand blood revenge on the spot.

"Claude," he murmured. "Claude Lacomte."

Sophie knew he caught sight of her tonsils before she managed to shut her mouth. His flaring eyebrows lifted.

"The name astonishes you?"

"Uh . . . yes. You're the cook I'm supposed to pick up and give the VIP tour before you meet the station brass."

Chef! You're supposed to call him a chef! Sophie put her foot in her mouth far too often for a woman who had once planned to join the diplomatic corps.

The green eyes widened slightly as they traveled down Sophie's compact form, a form which, at five-two, she determinedly described as average rather than short. Greer's tallness was a source of constant worry to Sophie. Could an anchorwoman be taken seriously if she had to put a pillow on the news desk chair?

"And you're not Greer Delaney!"

"Well no. There's a fire, you see. And Greer had to cover it. I'm her assistant, though."

Sophie drew herself up importantly. She might have a tough time seeing things at parades but no one could beat her at dodging under elbows in a reporter's scrum. Claude's lips pursed slightly, making Sophie hope his dignity wasn't offended by the substitution. Sexy lips, an inner voice added gratuitously as Sophie followed their movement for a fascinated second.

"Actually, you seem more surprised than me."

"Well . . . uh, yes." Sophie blinked out of her contemplation. "You don't exactly fit my idea of a cook. I mean chef."

"How don't I fit?"

His words were soft and dangerously leading as he waited for Sophie to trip up again. She remembered the jolly type she'd been expecting, rotund from ingesting massive quantities of cholesterol, red face permanently retaining heat from his ovens. "I thought you'd be . . . er, plumper. From sampling the goodies."

Despite an effort to look grim, the man's mouth twitched, quivered, then suddenly burst into laughter. In repose, something about the handsome face had suggested the austerity of a monk. Mirth instantly informed Sophie that the monk had long ago turned renegade, flinging over the rigors of religion for the myriad hedonistic pleasures of the here and now. The unexpected force of the revelation impacted shiveringly on Sophie's spine.

"You can't be faulted for lack of directness," Claude murmured, completely diverted from his wounded Porsche.

"And at least you're ... cheerful," Sophie seized advantage of the moment. "And we better get on with the tour. We can't afford to be late when the Buckeroo awaits."

Opening the door of her own car, she gestured grandly.

"You are licensed to drive on the street?"

"Any street in town. Hop in."

Tossing a mass of schedules aside, Sophie made room while Claude dubiously eyed the vehicle's assorted battle scars. He got in eventually and shut the door with a clunk that suggested a philosophical abandonment to fate.

"Where would you like to go first?" Sophie inquired as her car disengaged from the Porsche with an agonized squeal. Admirably, Claude kept himself from wincing.

"Show me your favorite spot in the city."

Sophie lifted her foot off the brake then put it slowly down again. No. No! she told herself. The poor sucker hasn't a clue what he's saying.

"My favorite spot?" she asked nevertheless, very distinctly, and with great innocence.

"I'd like to see Toronto from the point of view of a resident." The green eyes fixed her. "Most especially, you."

The ragged breath Sophie drew didn't have the least effect in stopping her. That green glimmer, hinting of the devil, drove her on.

"You're absolutely sure? Anywhere?"

"I leave it all up to you."

He smiled. An absolutely ... mesmerizing smile. A smile Sophie had no idea men were capable of. She blinked for a second, like a rabbit caught in the headlights, then recovered.

"All right. But just remember, it's where you asked to go."

As she pulled onto the street, a racing recklessness spilled through her, proof against all arguments of con-

science. Seize the opportunity was the first rule of reporting. A chance like this was simply too precious to let slip by unused.

To be fair, Sophie did give Claude a tour, a linear tour angling from Claude's lakefront hotel sharply northwest through the heart of the city. As they drove, she pointed out Bay Street, hub of the financial district; The Eaton Center, Toronto's huge downtown mall; the old and new city halls standing side by side, ornate Victorian redstone glowering at the sleek double curves of the usurper. Queen's Park, encompassing the massive provincial legislature buildings, sped by, as did the sprawling University of Toronto campus. At none of these places did Sophie slow the car or circle round for a different view. She did provide cheerful running commentary as they passed, chatter meant to be a disarming cover while Sophie exercised her journalistic skill on the man beside her. By nature, Sophie was more inquisitive than any ten ordinary citizens put together. Now, curiosity about her passenger had lodged itself under her skin with the intensity of a black fly itch—and Sophie set out to satisfy it as quickly as she could.

Before they had passed Bay Street, she knew he'd been born in Montreal, that he liked tennis, loved white-water canoeing, and that his preferred color was turquoise. By the time they reached City Hall, she knew that he'd had a chance at an NHL farm team and that he'd grown up in the hospitality business, helping his parents in their small hotel down Rue St. Catherine. By Queen's Park, he had revealed that he now owned the hotel in concert with his sister and that his parents had retired to the Gatineau hills. His sister ran the hotel while Claude, the restless one, searched out fresh fields to conquer.

"Sounds cushy. What on earth made you decide to try TV?"

Claude flung her an ironical glance.

"Why not?"

Off the cuff, Sophie could think of a dozen reasons why not, including lack of experience, lack of broadcast train-

ing, the notoriously fickle viewing audience, and the awful
pit that awaited this Claude should he fail. Kindly, she kept
her reservations to herself.

"Why not indeed," she returned lightly, smiling over
the steering wheel. "So tell me, are you single, married, or
all battered to bits by divorce?"

Sophie hung a left, cutting off a streetcar, a cement truck,
and a bicycle courier. Yet even as Claude clutched the door
to right himself, he didn't fall for the trick question camouflaged under a whopping distraction. A broad grin appeared.

"Now who could be interested in boring personal details
such as that!"

Amazingly, Sophie felt the beginnings of a blush. Her
heart skipped one beat, then two, waiting for Claude to give
himself away. He answered with such perverse, infuriating
silence that a gorgeous wife and three rosy children mate-
rialized in Sophie's mind. The picture filled her, inexplicably, with dismay.

"Nobody in particular," she shrugged, moving swiftly
to lull the interviewee. "Actually, I forgot what it was I
asked."

Claude sported two dimples on the left side of his face,
giving a raffishly wicked quirk to his humor. His eyes were
altogether too knowing. And too pleased.

"I think not. You've already managed to extract more
information from me in the shortest possible time of anyone
I've ever met. Greer Delaney had better keep her eye on
you!"

Flattery was flattery and Sophie'd take it anywhere she
could get it. She chuckled aloud.

"The Buckeroo is going to like you."

"And who, might I ask, is the Buckeroo?"

"The biggest cheese in the dairy. The boss. Just like him
to take a wild flyer on a cooking show."

"Do I sense a hint of newsroom condescension for my
chosen line of work?"

He had one eyebrow up and one elbow out of the window—a tableau so engaging that Sophie took her eyes off the traffic to watch the wind plucking at the hair along his temples. No way, she decided, that a family man could look as rakish as that. And the Porsche, she now remembered, had only two very low bucket seats. Heartened, she again resorted to her own charm, which was considerable when she chose to turn it on.

"I know absolutely nothing about cooking shows, so how could I judge? Myself, I have trouble making a creditable pot of tea."

Privately, she'd rather be dropped overboard as bait in shark-infested waters than be stuck banging pots around.

As they left the older part of the city, Sophie's attention shifted toward their destination. She hummed with a galloping exhilaration compounded by the freedom she had just grabbed for herself and, admit it, the presence in the seat beside her of a most delectable hunk. She ran a yellow light, just managing to cross a throughway before the opposite stream of traffic surged forward. Claude gripped the seat with two sets of knuckles.

"Always drive like this?" he inquired through his teeth.

Sophie prided herself on getting around the city as smartly as any cabbie on the run. "Of course. Why?"

"Oh, just a foolish interest in bodily survival. And aren't we sticking to one direction rather fanatically?"

"I guess we are."

Sophie couldn't even sound surprised. Even if she hadn't bamboozled Claude into giving her free rein, the car would have steered itself in this direction completely of its own volition. She returned to the problem of Claude's love life. Unrevealed information was worse than a pebble in a shoe. She could not rest until she got it out.

"Have you found a place to live in the city yet?"

"I'm looking at an apartment tomorrow. If it's suitable, I'll have my things shipped right away."

My things. Not *our* things!

A little pulse started up in Sophie's throat as she waited for Claude to elaborate, but he appeared to have clammed up. Perhaps she had hit a sore point. Some involvement he wanted to keep to himself—or even a scandal not quite buried. Surreptitiously, Sophie examined her companion again. Those eyes! Those maddeningly one-sided double dimples! Yes, she could imagine him blithely hopping from one spot of trouble to the next. Women would . . .

A diesel tanker snorted past within a foot and half of the bumper, causing Sophie to jerk out of her speculation abruptly. She'd better leave Claude's private life alone or she'd end up wrapped around a bridge abutment. There'd be time. Oh yes, plenty of time for probing later on.

Unconsciously smiling, Sophie swung directly north and stepped on the gas. They were now heading into the region of the vast, faceless housing tracts. As they grew closer to their destination, Sophie's eyes began to gleam with anticipation and her breath became faster. She beat one traffic light after another and instinctively skirted streets blocked off by a police car.

"Where are we going?" Claude asked, picking up both Sophie's animation and the disturbed traffic in the area.

"My favorite spot! To watch the CAM news team in action."

Unerringly, Sophie found a back lane and booted past the last obstacles blocking the way. Claude audibly caught his breath.

"My god! Half the subdivision must be on fire!"

It did look that way, with clouds of acrid smoke billowing into the sky and columns of flame spurting from the plywood and framing of the half-built houses crowning the rise in front of them. Sophie herself was taken aback, though she covered at once.

"Oh, don't worry. There was nobody in it. Greer and the news crew will be somewhere near the center of the blaze."

As though she did it every day, Sophie swung into the mass of police cars, fire trucks, and spectators clogging the scene. When the car's grille scraped a police barricade, she switched off the motor and hopped out. Dubiously, Claude followed.

"Here's the lowdown," Sophie said rapidly, catching his arm—which she could not help noticing was firm and hard under her fingers. "This project got started before the building permit was properly finalized. Hooper Developments was hot to cash in while the Toronto housing market was skyrocketing and figured no one could say no after the houses were practically up. The skulduggery at City Hall alone would fill a volume, not to mention rumors of payoffs on the sidelines, graft among the suppliers, shoddy workmanship, and so on. A second group claims the land belongs to that ravine over there, a nature reserve. They've been lying down in front of cement trucks and threatening much worse if the grass and trees aren't put back immediately. The original owners of the land, a couple of dear old revolutionaries in their eighties, claim they were swindled on the purchase deal and want legal redress at once. The local architects voted it ugliest design of the year. And just last week," Sophie spread her hands as though she could not encompass such a cornucopia of juicy scandal, "work stopped altogether. With all the foul-ups, not a house has been sold. Hooper must be just about bankrupt!"

"So?" Claude looked at Sophie obtusely.

"So! Don't you see?"

"I see a lot of good lumber going up in flames."

Sophie almost grabbed his lapels before stopping herself.

"The tip to the station today said the fire looked deliberately set. That means either Hooper is trying to recoup his losses through insurance or the environmentalists mean to make sure no other outfit snaps up the place at a bargain and goes on to make a bundle."

"And the octogenarian revolutionaries?"

"Not to be discounted. They spent most of the thirties in and out of jail for union activism and civil disobedience. Oh I can't wait for the fire marshal's reports to come in!"

Rapture was the only word for Sophie's expression as police pushed spectators back and firemen slogged through

raw muck, dragging heavy hoses. Despite her assertive fa-
cade, this was the biggest news event Sophie had ever been
to and certainly the first outside the CAM building. All
those practice assignments in journalism school were nothing, she realized with a thrill, absolutely nothing to the real
thing. Oh how she needed field experience, practice speaking off the cuff, cornering the key players in the heat of
the moment. She'd be in seventh heaven if she could just
pick out some angle Greer had overlooked and get it on
the evening news!

"Let's go find Greer and the crew!"

"But that's a police line!" Claude protested as Sophie
ducked under a ribbon of yellow tape.

Pityingly, Sophie looked back at him.

"No one ever got a story by respecting police lines. Besides, we're press. And I think that's our crew over there."

If they got stopped, Sophie knew she could do a good
bluff. Once they made it to the CAM crew, they'd be safely
with their own—providing Greer didn't have them arrested
first. Leaping hoses, dodging between fire trucks, they
made it a good part of the way before Sophie stopped short
and ducked sideways.

"CXRT," she explained, pointed out a second news
crew. "Our arch rivals. You'd better get used to hearing
about them around the station. There'll be a knock-down-
drag-out slugfest over who airs the best coverage tonight."

"That competitive?"

Could the lad be such a lamb in the media woods as
that?

"Better believe it. Their budget makes ours look like
pocket money. The Buckeroo takes particular delight in
rolling over them whenever he can."

Sophie started forward again, tugging Claude, detouring
to avoid CXRT. Scurrying, they passed more firefighters.

"Keep your head down," Sophie ordered, not knowing
whether Claude would try to bolt back to the car. After all,
he was getting grit all over his fine European loafers.

A policeman spotted them and yelled, "Hey!" furiously.

Before he could head them off, Sophie did a quick turn and
sped around a half-collapsed construction hoarding. She
crouched for a moment, hair tumbling over her eyes, breath
coming in swift, eager pants at the excitement of the game.
Claude looked down at her as she sighted the CAM crew
again beyond the obstacle course of ditches and construction equipment. His expression had changed from confused
chagrin to unbelieving fascination.

"By the way," he began as though on sudden impulse,
"you wanted to know . . ."

The rest was lost as Sophie made a sudden dash for the
cover of a resting bulldozer.

"Know what?" she asked as Claude skidded to a halt
behind her. She still gripped his wrist tightly lest he try to
escape.

"My . . . marital status. . . ."

The words jumped unintentionally, because Sophie chose
that exact second to dart toward the back of a ladder truck.
She hadn't quite reached it when the words registered.

"What?"

Not expecting her to halt screechingly while still in the
open, Claude slammed into her from behind. Sophie stumbled sideways, her foot tangling in a length of fire hose.
The jerk of her weight tore the hose from the grip of the
fireman directing it. The powerful jet dropped earthward,
bounced once, then began to twist and snake with a mad
life of its own.

"I'm . . ."

"Look out!" Sophie shrieked, quite uselessly. A strong
arm flew around her ribs and lifted her from the ground. It
was a heroic effort, truly heroic on Claude's part, to get
them back behind the bulldozer. It did no good whatsoever.
The firehose caught them in its blast, knocked them flat,
and held them there till three burly firefighters wrestled the
hissing water under control.

Chapter Two

"Sophie! Come quick!"

Dropping the latest Peruvian trade statistics on their head, Sophie galloped into the living room of the flat she and Agnes shared. That cry meant there was something on TV no aspiring newsperson could miss. CXRT was running "Show Bits," its nightly half hour of entertainment news, reviews, TV gossip, and sizzling scoops. Agnes was addicted to the thing, often chiding Sophie for disdaining the juicy bits of fluff. Especially rich were the visits of Lola Mallow, professional gossip monger, for lack of a better term, who not only wrote for the local papers but held down a spot on "Show Bits" as well as showing up regularly in magazines, on radio, and probably in static on the telephone wires. Where she managed to get so much inside information had been a source of fascinated speculation for years.

When Sophie arrived, Lola was already eyeing the camera, glossed lips parted in that intimate, knowing way that gave such credence to her lightest insinuation. She was a woman of the Buckeroo's vintage who had managed to turn the term "well preserved" into a verb with her endlessly evolving hair colors, her openly publicized lifts, tucks, and smoothings, and her Garbo lashes shading shrewd black eyes. If she did not exactly wear leopard-spot turbans and chandelier earrings, she gave the perpetual impression of being so attired.

"... and Claude Lacomte, host of CAM TV's new gour-

19

met show, will be on the air just as soon as CAM can rush some tapes to completion. CXRT's news crew caught a sneak preview glimpse of the celebrity during a surprise appearance yesterday at the site of the Hooper Developments fire. . . ."

Lola's eyes gleamed for a moment before the screen switched to a clip which caught Claude and Sophie almost at the exact moment the fire hose hit them. Sophie saw herself stop, look up at Claude, stumble, then shriek soundlessly. Claude, in one swift motion, scooped her against him even as the stream of water slammed them both backwards into the mud. The clip faded. Lola reappeared, looking, as she always did, as though there were volumes more to be told should she care to indulge.

"Rather a damp start to Claude's television career. Let's hope he's not so all wet when his new show goes to air. Of course," Lola grinned catlike, "he might have engineered the whole episode just to get his arms round his pretty companion. Sophie Moore, we have discovered, is an assistant in the newsroom at CAM, so we know they'll be seeing more of each other. Trust "Show Bits" to keep you up to date. . . ."

Lola, in turn, faded into a toothpaste commercial while Sophie stood frozen, a hand pressed to her mouth. Agnes was doing the same—trying to suppress mirth within. Even Sophie's shock couldn't squelch her. She burst into loud guffaws.

"Oh Sophie, I'm sorry. But you set yourself up for that. And Lola gets points for recognizing a hot one when she saw it."

Sophie remained rigid, cataclysmic thoughts crashing through her head—all of them to do with the Buckeroo's reaction to the clip. Jock Owen particularly detested Lola Mallow and hated being the object of her darts. Lola, in turn, never lost an opportunity to skewer CAM if she could possibly get away with it. Not only was this the result of the intense rivalry between the stations, but rumor had it that, way back in the Dark Ages, Jock and Lola had once been an item, parting explosively. Nobody knew for sure, of course, but after one of Lola's gleeful hatchet jobs, the Buckeroo would storm about, prodding his staff to, somehow, some way, get the jump on CXRT. The gourmet show itself was a result of this antagonism. When Jock's spies informed him that CXRT had written one into their upcoming schedule, Jock had hired Claude almost instantly to beat his rival to the draw.

Sophie took a pace distractedly.

"Oh, I was so sure everything got smoothed over. The Buckeroo will be livid!"

"Maybe he won't even notice!"

"Are you kidding! He's as obsessive about 'Show Bits' as you are! And if he missed it tonight, there's a dozen people who'll make sure he gets a copy in half an hour!"

"Including Claude Lacomte?"

Sophie shivered, imagining Claude's reaction. Agnes narrowed her gaze.

"Last night you said you had it sorted out."

Sophie began to gnaw at the ends of her hair, a sure sign of agitation. She had chin-length hair so brown as to appear black to the undiscerning eye. That combined with blueness of eye and paleness of skin instantly gave away a wild black Irish ancestry.

"Come on, Sophie. Out with it. What really happened after Claude got soaked?"

After a few restless steps, Sophie shoved her hair back and emitted a whoosh of breath.

"He seemed so good-natured. Really, Agnes, he did. He didn't get mad when I dented his fancy car. He hardly protested when I whisked him straight to the fire. But whew! I sure hit his limit when I dragged him in front that fire hose!"

Of course it had been an awful shock to be knocked flying by a high-pressure jet—but even then Sophie had been proud of her quick wits. The second she stopped slithering, she had hauled Claude behind a pumper. She'd been convinced, absolutely convinced, that no one from the news teams had spotted them in that mass of shouting confusion. The CXRT camera must have caught them on a blind scan and someone had had the incredible sharpness to pick Claude out.

"He got angry?" Agnes asked.

"Angry! He went up like First of July fireworks! And he didn't cool down even when I explained there was plenty of time for us to go back and change before he had to meet the Buckeroo."

"My, what a poor sport. And I suppose he soaked your car upholstery too."

Sophie paraded to their living room window, then back again.

"Don't make fun, Agnes. He really did look nice when I finally got him to the station door.

"Nice, but still mad?"

"Well, a little . . . odd." Sophie spread her hands. "I didn't know what to make of him."

She'd guessed right about the volatile temper. It had quietly stretched all afternoon, then gone up suddenly in a pinwheel of bilingual expletives. He'd not only been angry, but utterly incredulous when, even in her sodden state, Sophie hadn't wanted to leave the fire. Longing had been naked in her face as she watched an aerial truck edge up to a roof agush with flame.

"Biggest local story we've had in months," she told him, twisting round inside the car. "I almost got to go legitimately."

"But got collared to baby-sit me!"

Sophie had pressed her lips together hard, for she was hanging between water-shock, appeasement, and an irrational flare of temper of her own.

"I enjoyed taking you for the drive."

The statement was so tightly prim, so crazily at odds with their water-logged condition that Claude sat motionless while several muscles worked in his face. He looked down at his shoes, now oozing mud, at the haze of smoke penetrating the interior of the car, at Sophie's notebook still lying on the dash, open to the information about Claude's Porsche. The formidable fury vanished as quickly as it had appeared.

"Oh, tell me another!'' he had choked. His shoulders shook soundlessly for a moment, then he burst into a yelp of laughter that sent his wet hair flying and revealed a disconcertingly distinct torso under his semitransparent shirt.

While Sophie tried to take in this about-face, one corner of Claude's mouth quirked down, nicely ornamented with water drops. The rest of Claude's expression was a shifting mix of sternness, mirth, and residual temper—as though Claude himself didn't quite know how to put his mood together.

"Look, generally I'm an easygoing guy, but I do have my limits. You managed to reach them in less than an hour. That's a record for anyone but the wine waiter back at my hotel. And you're as wet as I am.''

That was very wet. Sophie could hear Claude squelch as he shifted to look at his watch, luckily a waterproof model.

"We have to move fast,'' he put in briskly, "if we're going to get ourselves dried out and presentable. We'll get downtown without too much risk to life and limb if you hang a right when we get to the lights and hit the Allen Expressway.''

Halfway to the car key, Sophie stopped.

"How do you know that? I thought you just got here.''

"I'm from Montreal, not the moon. I've been coming to Toronto all my life.''

"But I just took you . . .''

Sophie halted, thinking it not politic to mention the makeshift tour.

"You brought me to a disaster area and turned me into a disaster too. I'm just glad there wasn't an erupting volcano or a hurricane within driving distance. I mightn't have survived to tell the tale!''

A tiny, intriguing rivulet of water traced its way down the side of Claude's neck and vanished into his shirt collar. Warily, out of the corner of her eye, Sophie watched its progress. She knew for sure that he wasn't nearly so easy-going as he claimed. She particularly wouldn't like to work for the fellow. Nevertheless, a good journalist never left without all the facts. She slewed her car over the raw construction track and stopped just before the rear wheels hit pavement.

"You never did finish whatever you were saying out there."

The green eyes met hers, startled, then brilliantly agleam with something Sophie couldn't read.

"Single," he exclaimed. "End of sentence!"

Sophie stepped on the gas and soon after, delivered Claude to the station at last, clean, dry, and handsome. And felt altogether too relieved over at least that part of her duty faithfully done.

"The question is," Agnes mused, "how much trouble is Claude going to get you in over this?"

"I've no idea. He's pretty unpredictable—especially under pressure."

"Of a fire hose, for instance. . . ."

Agnes intercepted the pillow Sophie flung and tucked it behind her head.

"Look, chefs are supposed to be temperamental. Did you know that, years ago, the most famous chef in France once committed suicide because the fish course didn't arrive on time?"

"You're putting me on."

"I am not. I had to do all this reading up for the bicentennial of the French Revolution. Another one invented Peach Melba so he could make time with an opera singer. Yet another ran a Paris restaurant famous for gourmet rabbit for years. It wasn't until they found all the cat skeletons in the catacombs under the place that they figured out how he managed the most unique ragout in town!"

"Gross!"

"So will Claude rake you over the coals to the Buckeroo?"

Gnawing another strand of hair, Sophie considered the

question. Sickly, she realized what a vulnerable position she was in should a new favorite, of semicelebrity status, such as Claude, choose to trash her. The Buckeroo hired and fired as capriciously as he did everything else. Sophie wouldn't mind being yelled at, for a journalist needed skin tough as a crocodile's. But if she ever lost this precious job . . .

She made a mental note never again to take a civilian with her onto the field of battle. Especially not when in Beirut.

"He did behave well over the fender bender," she conceded. "And if he tries to burn me on this, I can argue that he agreed to go to the fire. I was acting on his own instructions. Can I help it if my favorite place was a burning subdivision?"

She made another worried circuit of the tiny living room, then halted. Claude might be volatile, unpredictable, and, on good days, a dangerously charming devil, but she sincerely hoped he was not the type to thirst for revenge.

"Yeah, I can see the Buckeroo falling for that!"

"Well, it's true! He just wanted to see where I'd take him."

"You never told me that little detail," Agnes put in, her eyes narrowing with interest. "Sounds as though the great Claude took a bit of a shine to you."

Absurd, Sophie thought, even as a queer spasm feathered through her. Momentarily, her mind drowned in a flood of images from yesterday. The flicker of double dimples, that infectious, unexpected laughter, the wet shirt outlining all those interesting muscles, the soaked strands of hair making Claude look like a swimmer just emerged from some turbulent sea.

"Certainly not!" she sputtered—too vehemently.

Agnes's eyes grew even brighter and more birdlike. When she was really fascinated by something, she could look like a huge barn owl and she was looking exceedingly owlish now.

"Methinks the lady doth protest too much. And over a

most toothsome piece of manhood. Maybe Lola hit the money after all!''

Again, Sophie felt heat in her cheeks. She who took pride in never blushing!

"You know very well I haven't time to get interested in men. Nor you either. We've things to do and places to go. And both of us are barely on our way.''

Agnes sprawled across the sofa, a lifetime of friendship and familiarity between herself and Sophie. They'd been infants in the sandbox together. Side by side, they'd survived the agonies and ecstasies of high school. Drunk with escape, they'd fled small-town Ontario for the same big-city campus.

"Right! You're going to get the national anchor desk and I still have to write the Great Canadian Novel. We're going to be busy girls for the next twenty years!''

"Well, it's true, isn't it? Neither one of us has time to spare for men," Sophie exclaimed, surprised by the new asperity in Agnes's tone. Agnes simply grinned at her.

"That situation might change in a flash—should we find that men have time for us!''

She shifted the pillow to her bosom and hugged it melodramatically. Sophie burst into giggles.

"At least the pillow is an improvement on Aldus Winkler the freeloading tone poet. He nearly ate us out of house and home our freshman year. I thought you'd never get rid of him.''

"Ha!'' Agnes cried. "Might I mention Harry Tate, who dragged you out to all those rhumba lessons. And Stukey Talbot, the stock car racer who, heaven help us, taught you to drive. And Brian Hanes, with the super ego and the Super 8 camera. And Stan! You barely, just baaarely, saved yourself from him!''

"Yeah.'' Even ebullient Sophie sobered at the mention of Stan Winterly. She had a close call on that one. A very close call. It had put a prudent end to romantic adventuring and turned her attention firmly to her work.

Agnes sprawled full length on the sofa while Sophie

28   *Gail Hamilton*

cheeks. This signal dated from kindergarten, when Agnes had fallen madly for her finger-painting partner.

"Of course not. Just because he reads Proust is no reason he should have anything to do with anything!"

Nellie entwined herself about Sophie's legs as Sophie considered this wide-open opportunity to tease her friend. How odd that she couldn't find the inclination—or any of the dozen merry darts usually at her command. How odd she could only see Claude Lacomte's face—looking ironic.

Slowly, Sophie rose to her feet, relieved to discover that Agnes's probing was just a symptom of Agnes's own entanglements and nothing whatever to do with a certain handsome Quebecois. Her own self-image remained undisturbed. She was still a high-speed, fast-paced, sharp-thinking lady whose schedule was far too busy to allow for any silly dalliance under the moon.

"Mercifully for you," she informed Agnes, "I have got to go to bed. I've got a tough day tomorrow. But if I live through it, I'm going to give the third degree to this admirer of yours! Nobody messes with my roommate unless I approve!"

The fallout from the "Show Bits" clip was swift and immediate, though it came from Greer and not, as Sophie had feared, from the Buckeroo. It began when she arrived at the newsroom to find conversation stopped and everyone staring at her with uncomfortably keen amusement.

Uh-oh! she thought, sliding as unobtrusively as possible to her desk. She could already feel, breathing down her neck, those three dozen journalism graduates she had beaten out for this job.

"Sophie," Greer called. "Step into my office, please."

That Greer had a real office with a real office door was a sign of her high status around space-starved CAM. Sophie marched in, prepared for fight, flight, or some very fast explaining.

"Look, I'm really sorry about the CXRT clip. I thought I dragged Claude away from all the cameras right away."

Greer regarded Sophie over the little half-moon glasses

draped herself over the wicker chair which had one leg shredded to ribbons by Nellie, their cat. Agnes regarded her friend with suddenly quizzical eyes.

"What if it did happen?" she asked quietly. "For real."

"What?"

"You know what! The big one. Love."

Something in the way Agnes said the word so gingerly caused Sophie to grow attentive in turn.

"What's brought all this on?"

"Oh, just idle speculation. And the way you bounded in all sizzling from your encounter with Claude Lacomte."

"Look," Sophie grew suddenly businesslike. "I have to work my way up at CAM—provided I don't get fired for nearly drowning the new chef. Then I have to make an upwardly mobile move to a larger station. And a larger one after that. Then there's all the time I'll have to put in as a foreign correspondent, living out of a rucksack, dodging bombs. When I get back here and get my own anchor desk, and when you've got that novel done, then—only then— we might start thinking about such luxuries as men."

Agnes pulled a comically mournful face.

"Good grief! We'll be hoary as trolls by then! We won't even be able to snag one of the Seven Dwarfs!"

"Don't go philosophical on me or I'll have to take cover. Whatever happened to the mature, attractive career woman who fits everything into its place—including romance?"

"She gets in some practice along the way. Wouldn't hurt for us to try it too."

"Us?" Sophie inquired.

"I mean you!"

Several large pieces fell together with a clank in Sophie' brain. Grinning evilly, she hitched her chair toward h friend.

"This wouldn't have anything to do with Sid, the n weatherman, would it? He's been making bomber pas by your desk for the last three weeks."

Jackpot! Two bright flags of color flared on Agn

she only wore in the privacy of her own office. It was at times like these that Sophie felt most acutely her own short-comings beside Greer's highly polished self. Greer was Sophie's ideal in the whole world as far as professional image. She was also Sophie's despair when it came to imitation.

Greer had blond hair that settled by itself into its sleek, moussed curve. Sophie's hair, though very thick, had such fineness no style could tame the myriad tendrils that insisted on fighting loose. And as for clothes, Sophie knew better than even to think about copying the creations that hung so grandly on Greer's angular form. Besides being short, Sophie's figure tended far more to hourglass lushness than the lean modern woman on the run. Not really interested in clothes per se, Sophie nevertheless spent hours of agonized discussion with Agnes over how to dress for the camera. Fashion trouble Sophie considered far more serious than a bit of clumsiness, for it affected how she was perceived. She was intelligent enough to realize that no matter how much substance, depth, and insight she projected, she wouldn't be taken seriously unless she looked the part too.

"I've already spoken to Claude."

"Oh." Incriminated, no doubt, to the eyeballs, Sophie braced for the blast.

"He said he asked you to take him anywhere you wanted."

Ah, well! Sophie allowed herself a twitch of optimism, noting that Greer didn't have that killer gleam she got when a corrupt city councillor squirmed on her hook.

"The fire was my first choice. Naturally, I took him . . ."

"Yes," Greer cut in, "you took him. So the responsibility for this debacle lies completely with you."

Sophie swallowed, but didn't abandon her effort to seem a legitimate member of the field crew. She believed in the principle of acting the role of who you really wanted to be, and sooner or later it was bound to come true. Greer peered skeptically over the half moons, and continued.

"Needless to say, Mr. Lacomte is a bit shell-shocked

about such an introduction to the viewing audience—and I can't say as I blame him." Greer paused while Sophie stoutly resisted a compulsion to stare at her shoes. "Mr. Lacomte doesn't yet understand how the media game works. Or how many more people will be looking for his show because of that clip, unfortunate though it was. That is, if they still remember him three weeks down the line when his show is scheduled to go on the air."

"Three weeks!" Sophie croaked, forgetting all about her shoes. "No show can get on side in three weeks!"

Greer grinned, dissipating the tension in the room and making Sophie want to kiss the potted geranium in gratitude.

"You still don't know the Buckeroo. When he wants something, he wants it now. The time slots are waiting, the studio assigned, the crew booked. All that remains is for Claude the chef to put his set together the way he wants it and get on with the show."

"Wow! That's pressure. Who's directing him?"

"Nobody, really. Who around here knows anything about cooking shows? Martin Scorley is producer."

"Martin Scorley!" Sophie almost committed a verbal blooper big enough to ruin her miraculous escape. After an abortive early career as a prize fighter, Martin had become a crony of Jock's in the newspaper days, when they'd both done the sports. Following Jock gingerly into radio, then television, Martin had become a producer, with two wrestling shows, a fix-it series, and a game show involving water-filled balloons to his credit. His attitude to haute cuisine could easily be imagined!

"Kind of a joke on him by Jock, I think. And a way to give Claude a really free hand."

"Mr. Owen must have a lot of faith in Claude."

Sophie's tone spoke volumes about Claude's lack of media experience. Greer merely shrugged—then smiled at Sophie.

"Someday, if you manage to survive these fiascos, you really will make it to the action, Sophie. Underneath all the crashing about, you're pretty good. You've got the drive and the brains. Eventually, you might even have the judgment. Meanwhile, you have to serve your time back of the lines, like everybody else.''

But I've already served so much time! Sophie protested silently, thinking of all the years of school, the nights dreaming, the days studying till her eyes wouldn't focus. Her impatience rose up inside her and she had to bite it back hard in order to keep looking contrite. Greer began to frown again. Sophie edged prudently toward the door.

''Not so fast. There's penance. You're to find Claude and apologize—on behalf of the entire station. Explain that Lola is an occupational hazard he'll have to look out for. And you're responsible for paying for his ruined clothes!''

''His clothes,'' Sophie gasped. ''Why the shoes alone are worth a week of my salary. Then there's those expensive trousers and his leather jacket . . .''

Just the thought of the jacket made her weak in the knees. For all she knew it had been hand-stitched by Albanians and was worth more than her family's collected assets. She got no sympathy from Greer, who was already turning to her desk.

''Makes you think twice, doesn't it, about enticing some unsuspecting soul in front of a fire truck.''

''Well?'' Agnes demanded as Sophie marched past, altogether too hot in the face for comfort.

''Sackcloth and ashes, as I make the grand apology to Claude. And I have to cough up for the clothes trashed by the firehose.''

''But you didn't get canned!''

''No!'' Sophie brightened, for she was nothing if not resilient. ''I better go right now, before I have time to think about it, and find out the damage.''

She sought Claude in the east wing of the old building that housed CAM. As she trotted down the hall, several emotions flitted through her. Relief, annoyance, trepidation—and a renegade pleasure at this excuse to see Claude again so soon. She was so glad to still have her job that she could stand almost anything from him, even another barrage of bilingual cusses.

As she neared Studio E, where his show was to be taped, she fortified herself for what might await. Yesterday he had recovered his temper, even after the dreadful plastering. But yesterday, he hadn't known half the province would see his elegant self ignominiously splattered in the mud. Perhaps he had already evaporated from rage.

Ancient Studio E was already a mass of activity. Scaffolding lay in heaps, dust rose in spirals, and a tingle of excitement pervaded the air. The source of this tingle was Claude himself, shirt sleeves rolled up, deep in conference with Martin Scorley and two other people. All activity halted when Sophie appeared. Yesterday, she had just been a faceless junior, scurrying about. Today, everyone knew she was the woman who had half drowned Claude. An unrepentant part of Sophie took note. At least she was making an impact. Taking care not to hesitate, she approached Claude with the apparent unconcern—and bravado—of a naturalist approaching big game in the wild.

"Good morning," she said cheerily. And as her hand came up in greeting, it struck the three cardboard coffee cups perched on a ledge of wainscoting. They flew to the floor. Each exploded into a bomb of brown liquid as the impact blew the lids away. Claude was the one who ended up with hot, dripping ankles.

"Ah . . . excuse me a minute."

Martin Scorley, battered veteran of so many battles, decamped at once, leaving Sophie all alone with Claude.

"I came to apologize," Sophie began, her gesture including the current mishap, "on behalf of myself and the station and . . ." She paused, thrown off by Claude's immobility. "Aren't you going to dry you ankles?"

"When you're here, why bother? In a minute or two the plaster will fall out of the ceiling. Or I'll step on a live cable and the shock will dry my socks out nicely."

"You're angry, aren't you?"

Sophie had been fooled by his calm exterior. Now she

could see the telltale flush working up his jawline. The dandy speech she had rehearsed in the hall wasn't going to do any good. She wondered, with surprising regret, whether she'd ever again see those lopsided double dimples. Claude shrugged a shrug containing every acerbic atom of his Gallic ancestry.

"Me? Why should I be angry? I love to go on camera while wallowing about in the ditch!"

As he spoke, Claude pushed one of his sleeves up further. His arms, bared, looked quite as hard and strong as they had felt to Sophie yesterday, grasping her about the ribs. Claude regarded Sophie evenly through those thick lashes of his. He's building up to something, she thought. If I don't stop him, he might really blow his cork. Quickly, she sucked in a breath.

"Look, I was just saying, I got sent down here to apologize for what happened yesterday . . ."

"Sent?" Claude inquired, very quietly.

Uh-oh! Tactical error.

"Yes."

"Then I take it that you don't feel abject contrition in your heart of hearts yourself?"

"Well, it was an accident," Sophie burst out, forgetting her resolve to be calm. "You can't dispute that!"

"Not unless we count enticement and entrapment."

The words purred out so smoothly it took Sophie a good five seconds to catch their meaning. Her blood pressure shot up.

"For your information, that publicity you got is worth its weight in . . . in solid gold ratings! You couldn't buy it! Not with all the money in CAM. Now hundreds and hundreds of people know who you are and all about your show before you've even had one plank of the set put together. Mr. Owen himself should have made that clear when you told him about the—event at the fire!"

"What makes you think I told him?"

The green eyes bored into Sophie while one hand stroked the side of his chin.

"Well, you did, didn't you?"

"And tattle on my enterprising guide! Not I! The first Mr. Owen knew about it was when he turned on that woman with the yard-long eyelashes. Of course, he called me immediately."

"I see."

To discover that Claude really hadn't ratted on her deflated Sophie considerably. If she hadn't been so stirred up, she would even have found Claude's restraint . . . gratifying. Oh well, better get to the painful part right away.

"I'm to reimburse you for the clothes that got ruined. Just make up a statement and give it to me. I guess," her gaze slid to Claude's ankles, relieved to see he was wearing ordinary blue jeans, "that includes your current attire."

Claude remained silent so long Sophie began to shift from one foot to the other. It was tough enough offering to pay for a man's clothes without him looking at her as though she ought to buy him a new car too. Impatience got the best of her.

"Don't you want compensation?"

For a moment, Sophie could have sworn, she spotted the double dimples. Just a flicker, but a flicker full of more mischief than she had seen in a year. The green gaze dwelled on her intently, and seemed to grow smoky. Once again Sophie felt that unidentified spasm in her abdomen.

"Oh, I want compensation all right," the smooth voice husked out. "But I'll need a while to think of exactly what. Be here, same time, a week from today. My account will be ready then."

What had he meant! Sophie asked herself later, as she went about her round of gathering poll scores, transcribing interviews, distributing mail, and trying to sniff out, on her own, a story Greer might be interested in. She couldn't forget that flick of dimples, the brief, smoky heat of his gaze as it traveled over her face and rested for a fraction— one tingling fraction—upon her mouth. A completely inexplicable *anticipation* had surged over her. Anticipation? Over a clothing bill!

Nor could she miss the unaccustomed buzz about the station, a stir that reached even that heart of excitement, the newsroom itself. Ordinarily, the newsroom staff was so caught up in its own momentum that other happenings in the building rarely penetrated. Yet now there seemed a fresh breeze in the corridors, a bustle, and incredibly, sights of the Buckeroo striding about, humming horribly off-key show tunes to himself.

In short, Sophie's naturally inquisitive nature was being driven to distraction about what was going on in Studio E. Changes were happening, that much she knew. Changes at breakneck speed. The grapevine told her that Claude came early, worked late, and generally drove those associated with him like Atilla the Hun. Clearly, he was a man who, once he chose a thing, threw himself into it one hundred and ten percent. Sophie approved. It was how she had packed two years of journalism school into one. It must have been how Claude ran his hotel and led his team to win that gold medal in the Culinary Olympics.

Yet, curious as Sophie was, she made no foray to Studio E before the appointed day. For one thing, she was too busy—mostly due to whirlwind developments in the Hooper fire case. Arson, the fire marshall's report stated. Most definitely, though they were keeping mum about their suspects. Ellis Hooper proved slippery as a trout at avoiding press confrontations and even slipperier when cornered. Sophie got stuck with the major slogging through Hooper's corporate expenditures, recent business maneuvers, and general fast-footing about.

Also, though Sophie caught glimpses of Claude in the hall now and then, she wanted no chance encounter until the designated time. Something to do, she supposed, with mental preparation. She had been altogether too fascinated with the sight of him, striding along, confident, whistling softly as he went. Very pleased with what he was doing,

Sophie had guessed. Or else having a great time adding up the clothing damage in his head.

The appointed morning arrived. Sophie rechecked her bank account on the way to work and was not cheered by a routine press release stating that Toronto has just been designated the most expensive place to live in the western hemisphere.

"That must be why I could rattle my entire collected wealth in an empty matchbox," she told Agnes gloomily. "I sure hope Claude counts in depreciation on that bill."

So then why was she actually speeding toward Studio E! And why was she wearing her best new royal blue cotton sweater!

"My!" she breathed, stepping unexpectedly into a hive of carpenters at work.

Grotty old Studio E had received a paint job, a raised dais, and what actually looked like new flooring. Not only that, the back storerooms had been torn out. In their stead, curved rows of seats were being installed to form a compact amphitheater.

"Would you believe, a live audience," Max the floor manager laughed. "The Buckeroo has been watching too many talk shows."

"It's going to be taped like that?"

Max nodded, rolling his eyes. A live audience affected the taping enormously, for there could be no real retakes should anyone muff things or very little cut lest the show run under time. "And is this the kitchen?"

The center of the dais was being sculpted into a gleaming white and gold work center with built-in oven, countertop burners, angled counters, and ample storage space neatly within reach. Hooks hung overhead, and there were great shelves, perhaps for appliances, behind. The whole had a clean, futuristic look entirely at odds with the creaky old building.

"What are all these for?" Sophie pointed at the hooks.

"Who knows," Max sighed. "What Claude wants, Claude gets. You'd have to take a look at the plans."

Someone waved a clipboard, and Max hurried off.

"Impressed?" inquired a warm voice almost at her ear.

Sophie started. She hadn't seen Claude for days and, in the interval, had forgotten the impact of his physical presence. His breath feathered the back of her neck, provoking, from Sophie's body, an instant, involuntary reaction of happy greeting.

"Frankly, yes."

She examined Claude with some caution. His face appeared bland and this in itself was suspicious, for Claude did not have a face designed for blandness. He wore an open-necked shirt and had three file folders bunched under his arm. Only those green eyes betrayed his real self, those dangerous, unpredictable, very alive green eyes. Eyes a woman had better watch out for.

"Looks like you're planning a live audience. However did you get the Buckeroo to loosen up the funds?"

"It was his idea. Real give and take. Life for the show." CXRT must be doing something similar, Sophie thought privately.

"It'll put a lot of limits on you. No retakes, no covering up mistakes, very little editing possible because of length considerations. It's tantamount to being on live TV."

"And you're wondering if little old neophyte me is up to the challenge."

So much for blandness!

"Exactly," Sophie retorted pointedly. "What experience have you had in front of audiences? Can you field questions? Can you time your performance to the second? What are you going to do if your omelette boils over? And most of all, have you already fallen victim to the Buckeroo's grandiose scheming?"

Claude's mouth quirked—either amusement or offense.

"You get to the point, don't you?"

"In this business only the finished product counts. There's no time to pamper delicate egos."

Claude leaned on a spare carpenter's horse, displaying distinct ridges of muscle under the shoulder of his shirt.

"You're wondering if I'm going to make a fool of myself the very first day. More of a fool than I'm already made out to be."

Adroitly, Sophie avoided this bait.

"If you're going to work in TV, you better to get used to the rough and tumble. The competition is just dying to take pot shots. If your show's a success, the public will love you. If it's a flop, CXRT won't let us forget it for years."

"Thank you for the vote of confidence."

The dryness of Claude's reply could have shrunk a prune. Belatedly, Sophie realized that she ought to have kept her mouth firmly shut until after they had dealt with the reason she was there. She, after all, was the one flung upon Claude's mercy.

"Ahem, well . . . yes," she murmured, attempting to calm the conversation. She sighed at her own runaway tongue, then decided to be direct. "Anyway, I came when I was supposed to. Now, what do I owe you for the clothes?"

"Ah yes, our unfinished business."

Mischief leaped back into Claude's eyes. He leaned back on one leg, rubbed his chin, pursed his mouth, and generally gave a good imitation of profound consideration. Sophie tried to swallow unobtrusively, thinking of her emaciated bank account.

"Might have to be installments—if that's okay with you."

"Yes indeed," Claude returned. "I was going to suggest installments myself. What I demand is the rest of my city tour—starting right now with lunch!"

Chapter Three

"Lunch?" Sophie let her mouth pop wide open.

"Why, yes," Claude drawled. "That meal in the middle of the day. They do let you eat, don't they?"

Mostly they didn't. At that very moment, Sophie had four urgent projects on her desk, plus a dramatic break from the fire marshal's department. The Hooper fire had been started by, of all things, a Molotov cocktail. Very thirties. Immediately, Greer had assigned Sophie to dig up everything she could on Beatrice and Ivor McClosky, the elderly couple crying foul on the land deal. Also, Sophie was still walking a fairly thin line because of her previous fiasco with Claude. Yet, all unbidden, her pulse gave a surge at the thought of those green eyes regarding her intimately from across a restaurant table.

"Sure they do. Where do you want to go?"

Claude's chuckle was warmly disarming. Too late, Sophie developed a vision of some horrendously expensive hideaway where Claude could watch the bill drain the last penny from her credit card limit. Gritting her teeth, she calculated that it would still come out far cheaper than a straight clothing total.

"You choose," Claude said, not taking advantage of the opportunity. "I want to go to your absolute favorite lunch spot. And," the double dimples appeared, "perhaps we can make peace."

"My favorite lunch spot?" Sophie asked, incredulously.

Surely he didn't want to perch on her desk in the newsroom.

Claude's eyes crinkled and friendly lights glimmered through his lashes. He shrugged, the very picture of amiability.

"You lead, I follow. Put it down to research."

A horde of other people at the station would have fought to take Claude out—but he was asking Sophie. The very core of her started to grin despite the perilous déjà vu of Claude's request.

"I know just the place. Meet me in the lobby in half an hour."

In the washroom, Sophie was hastily dashing on makeup when Agnes slid up behind her.

"Shouldn't you be on the telephone tracking down McCloskys?"

"Mmmnnnn."

"Don't mumble. What's up?"

"How do you know something's up?" Sophie asked, working on her lashes.

"Because you're using your good mascara. Considering what you paid for it, I know you'd only wear it for the visit of Walter Cronkite or a prince of the realm."

"I'm taking Claude Lacomte out to lunch. As payment on his ruined clothes. Maybe, just maybe, I'm going to get off light."

"And that's why you're grinning from ear to ear."

"I am not!" Sophie protested, even as she discovered in the mirror that it was true. No matter how she tried to straighten her face, it sprang right back into its pleasurable set. "I guess saving money makes me happier than I thought. I know the price range of every establishment for ten blocks around!"

When Sophie met Claude, she saw he had donned a tie and had his jacket slung casually over his shoulder. He smiled at her, giving such full benefit of the double dimples that Sophie wondered seriously if the other Claude she knew, the one having apoplexy at the fire site, was a figment of her imagination. His healthy tan glowed and he was able to dominate the lobby even while merely leaning against a pillar by the door.

"Planning to lift an idea for your show?" she twitted, as they stepped into the summer sunshine.

His laugh reached out and seemed to touch her.

"Just tapping in to the jungle drums. Reporters are famous for ferreting out the real neighborhood eats!"

"Right!" returned Sophie, hearing of this for the first time, and tickled to be called a reporter. "I'm your shortcut?"

"Oh, I do want to have lunch with you. Choices reveal the person, don't you think?"

Several answers suggested themselves to Sophie but she supposed Claude was teasing her. It suddenly occurred to her—in the abstract, of course—that a woman who lived with Claude would have to get used to being teased. When he wasn't being drenched, humiliated on TV, and otherwise infuriated, he had this whole other side to him. Inquisitive, like Sophie, and inhabited by a brash imp who, very likely, could never leave well enough alone.

This idea troubled Sophie not in the least. As she swung along the sunny street, she found a mellow warmth spreading under her ribs. Must be the newsroom coffee, she supposed, that was making her feel so particularly fine. But then, who wouldn't feel fine on such a brilliant June day with the sun caressing the ornate old bricks around her, the sweet breeze dancing up from the lake, and the trees teeming with singing birds. When a woman paused admiringly as Claude strode by, Sophie realized it was her own breast that was full of singing birds. As soon as possible, she must have three more cups of that miraculous newsroom brew.

Claude, though he gave his usual impression of loping, had modified his stride so that Sophie didn't have to trot to keep up. Good! One thing Sophie detested was tall people who showed off their long legs by acting like antelope. For Claude, she decided, she'd pull out all the stops. She was taking him to Rita's, informally known as the Lead Spoon Grill.

And since Claude seemed to be keeping to his accommodating mood, perhaps they really could start their acquaintance over. From scratch, so to speak. This time Sophie would keep them on an even keel. No fire hoses, no spilled coffee, certainly nothing at Rita's that could possibly upset a soul.

Cheered at the prospect, Sophie began to notice how many of the women in the street gave Claude a second glance—sometimes even a third. Invitations hovered on faintly smiling lips, delicately slowed steps. But he's with me, Sophie chortled inwardly—and promptly looked so smug that old ladies chuckled, and two passing teenagers poked each other in the ribs.

Unerringly, Sophie crossed two side streets, negotiated a weedy lane, and emerged at Rita's. The restaurant squatted on the corner between a gas station and a tool rental depot. Fifties chrome and shiny black tile sheathed the outside, which was pitted and cracked. Dusty plastic rubber plants pressed against the windows, and the lettering of the sign had long ago blistered into shreds. Flinging open the door to all this splendor, Sophie stepped inside, inhaling the pungent scents with sighing satisfaction.

"Let's get a tray. Saves waiting for table service. If Rita's in a good mood, she'll slap on a pint of extra gravy."

The bouncy, floating energy that had propelled Sophie down the street, now carried her over to the self-serve line, where the tray rail snaked past a vast bank of steam tables. Above her, a speckled ceiling fan whirled, spreading the richly mingled aromas of cauliflower, black coffee, and hamburger grease. In the cavernous back, rows of commodious booths displayed their cracked vinyl seats, ketchup bottles, and jukebox selectors.

Claude remained on the threshold, apparently so overwhelmed by the scene that Sophie had to tug at his elbow.

"Come on. The mob from the tire plant will be here any minute and there won't be a scrap of meat loaf left!"

In seconds, Claude found himself pushing a battered tray behind Sophie, who was scanning the contents of the steam table hungrily. Fortunately, she missed entirely Claude's expression of disbelief as she loaded her plate. Limp broccoli, beans glistening greasily in the light, beef the color and texture of loose insulation, spongy buns, and, yes, a towering slice of marble cake smothered in gobs of synthetic icing and crowned by a cherry so permeated with red dye it probably winked in the dark.

"This has to hold me until after six," Sophie told Claude as she added fries, starchy soup, and a pyramid of crackers to soak in it. "At CAM you learn to load up whenever you get the chance. Besides, I have this amazing metabolism. I could eat a horse and never gain an ounce. Burn calories like a furnace. Doesn't matter what I put in, just so long as I get my volume every day!"

If Claude looked faintly queasy, Sophie never noticed. Though she certainly wasn't lacking in the appetite department, the little speech she had just tossed off was really meant to encourage Claude to follow her example with his tray. She wanted him to have a terrific lunch—and she wanted him to have it there. At Rita's, she could afford to pay even if Claude decided to eat his own weight in chicken à la king.

Midway along, they encountered Rita herself, ladling out mashed potatoes and gravy in the gargantuan quantities that gave the place its fanatical clientele. Resembling a Mack Truck unsuccessfully camouflaged by an apron, brick-faced Rita was really Sophie's idea of a cook. Rita took in Claude, winked vastly at Sophie, and added a fat cabbage roll to Sophie's plate.

"On me, pumpkin. Looks like you need your strength today!"

"Hi, Bert," Sophie said genially to the long-faced youth hunched over the cash register. "Both!"

Bert cast a mournful glance and rang up the total—a sum so startlingly modest that Sophie looked sharply at Claude's tray.

44 *Gail Hamilton*

"You've only got a bottle of mineral water!" she exclaimed in baffled tones. "Aren't you feeling well?"

"I was till I got here. . . ."

"Bert, get him some chicken soup. It's terrific for . . ."

"No, no, please. Just kidding," Claude put in hastily. "Let's go and sit down."

Paying up, Sophie led the way to a back booth, obviously her regular spot. She spent some moments transferring the contents of her tray to the scarred Formica tabletop, then slid into the seat with a happy sigh.

"I come here whenever I can. It's fast and it's friendly and the booths give you room to read the out-of-town papers."

Sophie picked up the ketchup bottle and shook great dollops all over her fries and cabbage roll, then sprinkled everything left visible with an encrustation of salt. Claude sat opposite, his gaze riveted to Sophie's plate as she tucked into the lot.

"Wonderful," she crooned as the first round hit her stomach. "I get so hungry sometimes in the office. Excitement makes me hungry. Today there was a lot of excitement."

"There was?"

As though unable to stop himself, Claude watched Sophie's fork travel from her plate to her mouth and back again.

"Oh, yes. That Hooper fire we were at? Well the fire marshal's report let out what kind of arson it was. Wait'll you see the fast footwork among the crowd trying to avoid the blame!"

Sophie continued to eat, but the action became entirely automatic as she was transported again to the hot-paced world of the newsroom, her eyes vivid, the tilt of her face enchanting. This flashing fire caught Claude up in spite of himself and he momentarily forgot about what Sophie was eating.

"Any clue as to who did it?"

"Oh, yes!" Sophie shifted with an air of confiding an

item of great import. "Somebody tossed a Molotov cocktail! Decidedly old-fashioned is what the fire marshal
said—for the arson trade."

"Old-fashioned? What do they mean, *old-fashioned*?"
A tendril of Sophie's hair quivered intriguingly in the
breeze from the ceiling fan. She added Worcestershire
sauce to her ketchup, and drew her brows together.

"Apparently, there are trends. That's one area I really
haven't looked into yet. Before the month is out, I better
do some real down-and-dig studying about it."

"About what?" Claude had lost his train of thought
again at the sight of the Worcestershire sauce. Not to mention that enticing tendril of dark hair.

"Arson. And how they investigate it. I mean, how do
they really tell how a fire started after the evidence has
been in an inferno for ten hours? Haven't you ever wondered about that?"

"Can't say as I have," Claude admitted, snapping the
top off his mineral water.

"Well I do, now that I've thought about it! Probably,
I'll stay awake at night until I find out." The bounce in
Sophie's speech implied that anyone with a scrap of interest
in life would be doing the same. Oblivious to the way
Claude examined his glass before pouring any of his drink
into it, she sped on, memories causing her face to soften
into a grin.

"My mom said I was the most curious child on the face
of the earth, always taking things apart, crawling under
people's porches, asking embarrassing questions, reading
The Gazette before I discovered Winnie-the-Pooh. You
know," Sophie laughed, "I once asked Mr. Wallace, he
was the president of our town council, whether he really
did suck lemons before every council meeting the way people said!"

Giving free rein to her ideas, Sophie was at her most
engaging. A dewy flush climbed her cheek and sparks of
inner brilliance diverted Claude momentarily from her eating habits. He soon gave in to his own curiosity.

"You're from a small town, then?"

"Oh yes. We didn't even have a crosswalk. Agnes and I—she's the station newswriter now—used to watch TV, read like demons—stacks and stacks of magazines—and dream of getting away into the big wide world outside. I guess I'm a classic case of wanting to make the great escape."

"Escape? What from?"

Sophie's lips curved provokingly.

"Nothing dreadful. I had a perfectly normal childhood, with a perfectly normal family. My mom and dad run the local hardware store and my brother wanted nothing but to go straight into the business after community college. I myself can assemble plumbing fixtures with the best of them."

"Nevertheless," Claude insisted, with subtle emphasis, "you wanted to get away. Why?"

Sophie was a natural talker, but she usually tried to restrain herself, at least on personal topics. Claude could be defined as a person she scarcely knew. Yet, sitting across from him, she might have known him for years, the way she wanted to run on about herself.

For the merest moment, she was silent, thinking of the story Claude didn't know. Small towns were warm and neighborly. Small towns could also smother you—and Sophie fought smothering the way a cat fights a blanket over its head. There had been nothing awry in her easy-going family except the complacency with which life ran on in its comfortable ruts, and the weight of expectation that Sophie would not deviate from the pattern. All through college, despite Sophie's strongest signals, they smilingly waited for her to come home to teach, perhaps, or start a pretty tea shop for the lucrative tourist trade. They were still waiting, she thought, expecting her to get over this newsroom passion any minute now. And then, in college, there had been that close call, that very close call with Stan . . .

Fortifying herself with a mouthful of broccoli, Sophie beamed up at Claude. "All the obvious reasons, including the desire to do the opposite of what everyone expected. I was always like that, I'm afraid. Plain perverse. Mom still teases me about a mix-up at the hospital when I was born. But the real reason is, I love the news. It's about everything important that goes on in the world. And the world," she paused intently, "is just so . . . interesting!"

"Your friend, Agnes, she's of the same stripe?"

Claude surreptitiously saved his glass of mineral water from one of Sophie's enthusiastic gestures.

"Just about. Only she wants to retire and write the Great Canadian Novel some day. In college, she studied literature."

"You too?"

"Oh no. Political science. Basic requirement if you're trying to make sense of the world. You see," Sophie's voice lowered confidingly, "for years and years I intended to go into the diplomatic corps. Maybe make ambassador someday. Wear beaded evening gowns and meet exiled archdukes and handle top secret, save-the-world negotiations. Heady stuff when you're fourteen."

The prospect of Sophie as an ambassador was too much even for Claude. He stopped with his mineral water halfway to his mouth. The double dimples twitched madly.

"You would have been lethal."

"I know," Sophie grinned between gulps of soda pop. "Anyway, everything changed inside of a day. I discovered the college newspaper, then the radio station. Right away, I was hooked! I can't describe it—that feeling of one's own words going out over the air to hundreds and hundreds of people. I got this . . . shiver deep down in my stomach, and nothing's been the same ever since. Took a sharp right turn into journalism school, packed two years into one, and presto! Here I am. Isn't life terrific!"

It was either Claude's presence or the recent carbohydrate loading that made Sophie feel so grand. And so comfortable talking about herself. The newsroom frenzy had melted into a beneficent glow rather like that one feels in a park, basking in the sun. Sophie simply enjoyed the sen-

sation, never wondering why Claude peered at her plate
from time to time so queerly.

"You work hard," he commented.

"Oh, sure I do. I know this is just a local station, but
you wouldn't believe the competition for my job. I'm
working my way up as fast as I can. I want to be a reporter.
I'd do practically anything to get in front of a camera."

She hadn't meant quite to say that aloud, but could not
hide the driving ambition hot in her eyes. She took a vo-
racious bite out of the bun lying by her plate, and looked,
somewhat comically, as though she would do the same to
anyone who got in her way.

"Really! I would!" she insisted earnestly. "Mud, rain,
sleet, fog, skulduggery at three in the morning, I don't
mind. All I need is one really good story to get me noticed."

She gestured again while Claude, forgetting he meant to
make his mineral water last, took a long, contemplative sip.

"Pardon me for asking, but, with all that education, how
come you're still delivering mail?"

"Ha! You certainly are green! It's a privilege to deliver
mail in the tiniest station. There had to be forty applicants
after my job, any one of whom would have gladly scrubbed
the halls on hands and knees. I've got a toe in the door.
Making it from there is strictly up to me!"

"Ah," Claude breathed, "that must be why you remind
me of a very charming human bulldozer. I'm glad I'm not
in your path."

"Me too," Sophie agreed cheerfully. "I've got to get
promoted to reporter, then jockey for a job at a bigger station as soon as I get some experience. I've everything
planned. See?"

Before she knew what she was doing, Sophie was using
her fork on the back of a napkin to sketch her rise in the
news world, face alive with energy and dreams. But when
she looked up, Claude was uncharacteristically silent. A
couple of sober lines Sophie hadn't seen bracketed his
mouth.

"What'll you do if something derails your plan?"

"Like what?" Sophie could not imagine anything short of irreversible brain damage that could possibly divert her.

A wry smile touched Claude's lips. He lifted one shoulder.

"Oh, I don't know. Suppose you met a man—and fell in love?"

Why were the green eyes suddenly so compelling, Sophie wondered. Why did the pit of her stomach feel she had just fallen off a roller coaster! The faintest finger of panic touched her and she forced herself to laugh lightly lest she fall victim to the danger, the temptation in Claude's look.

"Funny, Agnes talked about just that. Sid—the weatherman—he's been giving her the eye. And I believe she's weakening."

"Such a thing could never happen to you, of course."

For a moment, just one shivering moment, Sophie was able to imagine what it would feel like—to weaken. Quickly, she recovered her balance and smiled back with deliberateness.

"In good time, I suppose. Let's see," she made a show of counting on her fingers, "I'll have an opening for romance between the time I get called back from the foreign correspondent field and the time I campaign to get my own anchor desk."

"There'll be time for a family too, perhaps, in your very busy schedule?"

"Of course!" Sophie exclaimed forcefully. Despite all her career plans, it had never occurred to her that she wouldn't have a family. It was all a matter of timing. "Why do you ask?"

"Why do you think!" Claude replied, so softly Sophie thought she heard wrong.

A sudden, throbbing silence seemed to hang over the table while Claude's gaze rested on Sophie's face. A thick pulse stumbled inside her and her breath had trouble leaving her lungs. He couldn't be saying such a thing to her, he couldn't!

With apparent casualness, Claude watched the fleeting changes of expression as Sophie struggled heroically to contain herself. When her face grew still, he frowned slightly and seemed to change too.

"Just wanted to wish you luck," he added lightly. "When the time comes, I hope there's someone around with the same slot open in their calendar."

Oh, he was just teasing her! Nevertheless, something quiet in his voice, something tantalizing, even regretful, stopped up the heated retort rushing to Sophie's lips. Claude regarded her with unsettling directness, as though he were suddenly looking right through her, inside her. A hundred unspoken comments seemed to hang in the air.

For the first time, Sophie had a mental flash about the future, actually thought about it. She was certainly not against romance and marriage. Indeed, she was all for them, assuming that a husband and children would fit themselves neatly into her glamorous life—all in their own good time. Now, inexplicably, a yawning gap opened before her. What if no one showed up when she was ready? What if, after everything, she ended up alone—exactly the way Stan predicted when she had sent him packing!

The vision vanished as quickly as it had come, but it left a shaky sensation in Sophie's midriff. And what had got into Claude Lacomte that he felt compelled to pass that kind of judgment on her life? Sophie felt her spirit return in full—along with an overwhelming need to change the subject.

"You're only drinking mineral water," she pointed out, rather belatedly since he had been sipping slowly all the while Sophie made inroads on her plate. "You really feeling OK?"

"So long as I keep to mineral water. In here at least."

Sophie looked puzzled. Claude paused, then shifted closer, treating Sophie to a view of strong, tanned throat.

He had the look of a man who knows better, but just can't help himself.

"Hope you don't mind me asking," he inquired with an air of great scientific detachment, "but how can you actually eat those—things you have on your plate?"

"What things?" Sophie looked at her perfectly good entrée, then realized that something in Claude's face gritted each time she put a forkful in her mouth. "You mean this? It's fine, rib-sticking food. I have to fuel up whenever I get the chance."

"The broccoli is boiled to death, the beef stringy as old tires, and the gravy made from a synthetic mix. And to put ketchup on top! Appalling! Ketchup, by the way, is thirty percent sugar—not good for someone whose smile is their fortune."

"My, you have been restraining yourself," Sophie purred, piqued nonetheless. "It all tastes great to me."

"You mean you still have taste buds?"

"On duty, every one!"

Sophie grinned and chomped a gravy-sodden french fry.

"Surely you learned better in your home!"

"It's just like home," Sophie exclaimed nostalgically. "We lived on TV dinners, mostly, or something out of a can. Cleaner—no mess to mop up. Mom worked the store with dad, and she had to be very organized about running a family."

Was it her imagination, or did Claude start slightly?

"But you're from the country!" he protested. "In the middle of farms full of fresh produce. The very heart of home cooking!"

Sophie emitted a delighted squawk of laughter, nearly knocking her fork to the floor.

"Why Claude, I do believe you've been reading *Anne of Green Gables*! And you the big food expert. Don't you realize the modern world has come to the country too— and got rid of all that old-fashioned drudgery? Just before I was born we got a chain supermarket right in town—and I can tell you, that was an event. Free at last! Frozen dinners, cake mixes, instant mashed potatoes, toaster waffles, even the popcorn came pre-popped. No more slaving over hot stoves and boring ovens. Mom could make our favorite holiday dessert in about three seconds from these mini green marshmallows and pink spray-on whip. She . . . why are you staring at me like that?''

''Wouldn't you stare if you suddenly met a painted barbarian dancing around in the CAM lobby? With a diet like that, I'm surprised you're still walking upright, never mind managing to look so . . . er, pleasant. Don't you believe in nutrition?''

''Sure—for growing infants and skimpy lawns! My brother and I are both fine, healthy specimens, thank you very much!''

Claude fell silent rather too abruptly, making Sophie realize she had planted both elbows on the table and set her jaw aggressively. A certain firmness around Claude's mouth betokened an exasperation Sophie could already recognize. Belatedly, she remembered that he was the Buckeroo's pet celebrity and she couldn't afford to have him irritated with her.

''Anyway,'' she smiled, laying on a good dollop of charm, ''I'm lucky. Food isn't an issue with me. As Agnes says, I can thrive on rusty nails and boiled construction boots, just so long as I get enough. I've got a real newswoman's stomach.''

Pointedly, she polished off the rest of the marble cake, not neglecting a crumb of swirly icing. As she finished, Claude glanced at his watch, faintly startled.

''Much as I hate to break up this fascinating spectacle, I have to get back.''

Once outside, the warm sunshine, the rustling leaves, the laughter of playing children all danced around Sophie again, wiping away the stiffness of a moment before. On the walk back to the station, Claude fell silent, leaving time for his enigmatic words to play themselves again through Sophie's head.

You can't schedule love—that's what he had been saying.

So who had been trying?

She had—or at least assumed it would be there for the taking when she felt the need.

Need! A strange word to suddenly rattle about in Sophie's head! A strange word to persist at the same moment she realized that Claude always smelled of pine, that despite his urban roots, something about him suggested forests of evergreen and clean bracing wind. A tingle started inside her just at the sight of his long legs measuring themselves again to her step.

What if...

She refused to finish the rest of the speculation. Nevertheless, the singing birds started up again in Sophie's breast, trilling vigorously until she and Claude reached CAM. At just that moment, a young woman breezed up from the opposite direction, all but bumping into them as Claude reached for the door. Immediately, Claude halted, breaking into a welcoming smile that radiated pleasure directly upon this lissome creature.

"Oh, by the way, Sophie," he put in, turning back, "I don't think you've met my personal assistant, Marianne!"

Chapter Four

Caught up in final production, Claude vanished into his work again. No one would have dreamed of disturbing him. No one except Sophie, who did dream, at least once a night, of disturbing Claude spectacularly. Sometimes she stood alone in Studio E, applauding forcefully. Sometimes she fed him bits of green marshmallow across Rita's table. And once, cliché of clichés, she ran toward him, arms outstretched, through a field of scarlet poppies. She woke with a start each time, never quite remembering the details, but awash in images of double dimples and green, mocking eyes. All this so alarmed Sophie that she even gave up her regular binge of Galaxy Cakes before going to bed.

Mostly, Sophie couldn't forget the thud inside as Claude had introduced Marianne. A thud that had nothing to do with reason and everything to do with the fact that Marianne was fawn-eyed, rosebud-delicate, and instinctively chic in a way Sophie would never achieve in a hundred years of trying. Marianne had gone at once to Claude's side, tucking her arm about him.

"And so this green-eyed monster has enticed you out to lunch, has he?" Marianne had laughed, luscious French accents issuing from ripe lips. "Look out for him, or he'll be making you fall in love with him like all the other ladies he meets. It is enough that his audience is going to lose their hearts, without letting him create havoc around the station!"

Marianne was teasing outrageously, but with enough

confident meaning to extract an openly raffish grin from
Claude. Sophie had swallowed, suddenly making the con-
nection between the handsome chef and all the joyous music in her breast. Some primal sensor sprang to life, making
her feel like a new cat that has strolled by mistake into
another's territory. She was embarrassed to find herself
shaken with speculation about Claude and the lovely creature fitted under the crook of his arm.

Sophie made a point of shaking Marianne's hand—not
failing to note what a warm, slender, competent hand it
was. The bristling died. But when Sophie had left, the tingling sense of exclusivity she had had all through lunch
with Claude had melted away. Anyone, she supposed,
could be mesmerized momentarily by a pair of lop-sided
dimples and a laugh husky with intimacy. She was but one
of many. Why should she ever have supposed otherwise?

The odd sense of letdown persisted long after Sophie
parted from Claude, and her normally intense curiosity did
not incline to examine the phenomenon. Nothing, however,
was wrong with Sophie's inquisitiveness when it came to
Claude himself. Though isolated in the newsroom, Sophie
still managed to soak up all the rumor, scuttlebutt, and in-
house chitchat as Claude's show approached its premiere.
CAM offered tickets to the tapings. Almost instantly, lines
formed outside. Claude, for all his inexperience, proved
remarkably at ease before the camera, and worked on his
set with smooth, well-timed skill. This was a good thing.
There was no room for retakes. Even if there hadn't been
the problem of the live audience, the Buckeroo was tight
as bark to a birch when it came to shelling out for crew
and studio overtime.

The first shows went on the air with as much fanfare as
CAM could muster. The Buckeroo trotted about, beaming
with pleasure, having gotten the jump on the so far unseen
culinary show CXRT was said to be planning. Sophie and
Agnes suspended their Saturday morning to watch the premiere.

"My, my!" Agnes breathed after ten minutes—a single comment that somehow said it all.

The Claude Sophie saw on the screen was not in the least like the Claude she had come to know personally. He was precise, dexterous, and imposing, an intimidatingly white-coated master over a domain the likes of which Sophie had never before imagined.

"He's got more equipment than a NASA space lab," she cried. "How does he know what to do with it all?"

"Oh, he knows," Agnes replied, as Claude's hands magically built an impossibly complex concoction among the gleaming white and stainless steel all ground. Only his sudden, double-dimpled smile when he finished was familiar.

"Sure he knows. But nobody else but a rocket scientist could make any of that stuff he's putting together!"

"From the competition to get studio tickets, half the city is willing to try. You should see the feedback," Agnes said.

"Already?"

"Didn't I tell you not to kid yourself about what people are really watching? It's not the food, my dear. It's the delectable chef!"

Merry eyes filled Sophie's memory, and echoes of that laugh that could shiver a person's kneecaps.

"With a little help from Lola, no doubt," she added tartly. *And Marianne,* she added, to herself.

Lola hadn't missed the debut of "Ambrosia." Her remarks were telling, and archly to the point. "Who cares about the food," she crooned, "when Claude the chef is good enough to eat!"

Since tradition dictated that the staff got to devour the day's creations after the camera was switched off, Studio E became the most wildly popular spot at CAM. This culinary bonanza, which included dishes in the making, pre-cooked demonstration works, and assorted experiments, soon had everyone who could find an excuse jostling at the door. The only group left out were the newsroom people isolated at the other end of the building, too preoccupied, too far removed. While busily imagining Claude and

Marianne, heads together, planning show after show, Sophie managed to knock over the entire coatrack. As she picked it up, she lectured herself on the benefits of her seclusion. She hadn't, for instance, heard any more about Claude's ruined clothes. From the looks of it, she was getting off with merely the cost of a bottle of mineral water.

Claude, however, didn't forget the newsroom. One morning, at ten, the mail cart rattled jubilantly in. Atop the brown envelopes, a magnificent orange mocha cheesecake caught the light, eliciting a whoosh of breath from the staff.

"Compliments of Studio E, folks. Dig in!"

To say locusts descended upon the offering would have been an understatement. Everyone, even Greer, managed to score a piece, so that by the time Sophie, trapped behind the copy machine, fought through the crush, nothing remained but the box.

"Wasted on you anyway," Agnes grinned, licking the last icing off her lips. "Delicious!"

The others, in paroxysms of bliss, had no sympathy whatever. Sophie had, for once, failed to use her elbows swiftly enough. She pressed her lips together and suppressed a pang inside. A hunger pang, of course. She hadn't eaten since the malted milk and four dill pickles she had gulped for breakfast.

A happier newsroom returned to work while Sophie, in her disappointment, actually contemplated raiding the crumbs left on Agnes's desk. Instead, she applied herself to the McClosky file. The fascinating old firebrands had absorbed her completely. Their finest hours had been in the thirties, when they fought in the union movement. Fought, as far as Sophie could see, for a few scraps of dignity and a living wage in the face of brutal exploitation. Ivor McClosky had gone to war when the war came and returned with a bad limp and two medals and a near court martial for his peppery clashes with authority.

Sophie watched raw footage brought in when Alice and Luther had gone out to interview the tart and testy pair. They'd given Alice a hard time, their eyes still fierce amidst the wrinkled, papery frailty of the rest of them. Hooper had promised a nursing home and low-cost housing amidst his luxury units, a promise he broke the moment the deal was signed. No one as old as the McCloskys, he'd supposed, could possibly put up a fight.

Sophie had tracked down associates of the McCloskys, ancient themselves, who came to life at the name and told of unforgotten battles and help in the dead of winter when there was nothing to eat in the larder and not a dime for coal.

"Bea and Ivor are still alive then?" came the pleased question always. Sophie would always smile into the telephone.

"Oh yes. And still fighting, too."

By setting fires, she wondered, driven to extremity by Hooper's legal double-talk and their own inability to climb the barricades once more?

She was still thinking of the thin old pair when she slipped out to the water foundation. The last thing she expected was for Claude to appear beside her, his step so smooth and lithe she started at his suddenness. Despite the well-lit, familiar shabbiness of CAM, Claude could still give the impression of a tawny cat appearing suddenly out of the night. A frisson swept over Sophie. In spite of herself, she swallowed.

"How did you like the present I sent over?"

"Ha! In that den of wolves? I didn't even get a whiff."

Claude's expression lengthened into exaggerated chagrin.

"For shame! We'll need more drastic action—tonight at eight. Can you make it?"

Halting in mid step, Sophie peered up sharply to see whether the man was joking or not.

"After Rita's, I wasn't sure you were still talking to me."

A row of even white teeth appeared.

"I am—just barely. We still have a score to settle, remember. Only I can see I'll have to take over the tour myself. We'll go to a real restaurant tonight, and I'll try to introduce you to that strange, alien substance known as good food.''

Logic warned Sophie to beware even as something in her bosom did a ridiculous somersault. What was it about the man, she wondered, that could spread charm like some hypnotic essence in the air?

"Which restaurant?" she asked suspiciously.

"Mallory's"

Mallory's! Even Sophie recognized that one. It nestled in a former mansion north of Yorkville, so exclusive behind its Viennese shades that only the letter *M* announced its existence. It had the reputation of a hideaway where politicians, business heavies, entertainers, and the like could relax firmly out of the public eye. Deals were struck, unlikely partners met, all shrouded in the ultrareserved privacy that was Mallory's special cachet. Sophie longed to get inside its door simply for the people-watching—but she cringed at the thought of the astronomical price.

"Take the stark panic off your face," Claude put in. "You won't have to pay."

Honor dictated that Sophie protest about settling up her bill. But in the face of Sophie's emaciated bank account, honor didn't stand a chance. Claude looked sincere enough, though who could tell what he was really up to? And who cared, cried an exuberant little voice inside her. He was going to get her inside Mallory's. Maybe they could last out a whole hour together before the head-butting began again.

"In that case, I'll be ready with bells on." Sophie inundated Claude with one of her own high-voltage smiles. "Here's where you find me."

And as if she wasn't in enough of a whirl, Sophie stepped back into the newsroom as the phone rang. Being nearest, she answered. When she hung up, her eyes widened with the news.

"The McCloskys have been arrested for the arson of

Hooper Developments. They're taking them downtown now!''

Alice and Luther immediately went charging off to film the arrival of the old couple at the police division. Sophie itched to go along, but of course could not. She sank into her chair, her face fraught with speculation and dismay.

"That's solved then," Agnes sighed. "Who would have guessed!"

"They've been framed! I know it!"

"Right, Miss Marple!"

"Look, haven't I spent the past two weeks digging up background and going over the footage from the interviews? I can't believe they're arsonists!"

Agnes clucked her tongue warningly. "Hey, this is the newsroom. We don't get emotionally involved!"

She might have saved her breath. Sophie was already crackling with righteous indignation, chin set, objectivity fading rapidly from her horizon.

"Yeah, they made trouble in the thirties. Lots of trouble. Who wouldn't, when it was the choice between standing up for oneself and being treated worse than a galley slave?"

"And did anything happen to catch fire in the midst of these noble battles?" Agnes inquired.

Sophie pursed her lips. True, the odd abandoned building or overturned truck went up in smoke. Only to be expected when starving, unemployed people began to riot. Sophie had looked into the seamed old faces on tape and seen the heated pride. They would rant from street corners, but they would not set a cowardly fire.

"Well, it'll all come out in court," Agnes concluded. Supposing she had won her point, she returned to work. Sophie continued staring at the wall, wondering how the aged couple could possibly survive the ordeal of arrest and trial.

Greer wanted an immediate summary of all the information Sophie had dug up, and she leafed through the pages rapidly when Sophie brought the report into her office.

"What a life history," Greer exclaimed. "They were inciting riots back before my father was born. Whatever did they do when prosperity hit after the war?"

"Rescued abused animals, fought expressways, and generally made a hobby out of litigation. Then Ivor got arthritis pretty bad and they started keeping a low profile. The bit of land they sold to Hooper was their nest egg. Hooper got it way below its real value because he convinced them half his project would be housing for single parents and the elderly homeless. Of course he reneged the moment they signed."

"Are they sympathetic or just cranks?"

"Sympathetic," Sophie said promptly. "They took on Hooper in spite of his whole army of lawyers. You've got to admire them for keeping on slugging like that. Be a real shame if they're wrongfully convicted."

Greer assessed Sophie over her glasses. Belatedly, Sophie tried to look detached.

"If they did it," Greer said reprovingly, "they're guilty, no matter how old and dear they appear. Ivor hasn't been helping himself, all those shocking names he's been calling Hooper. I suppose they have several beloved old tabbies that will have to be put down if the McCloskys go to jail?"

"Actually, two nasty parrots and a bull terrier that's lost its tail to frostbite." Sophie was nothing if not thorough.

"How do you think CXRT will handle it?"

Joy welled up in Sophie at these unaccustomed questions. She was being taken more seriously, watched with an eye to more responsible duties. Claude, she thought irrationally, had just brought her luck!

Sophie dashed home, arriving just behind Agnes, who was feeding Nellie and ironing her best blouse. At Sophie's clatter, Agnes turned swiftly.

"All right, Ms. Moore! Out with it. You've been smirking like a drunken canary since three o'clock!"

"I have not!" Sophie protested, even as she realized the charge was likely true. "Anyway, Greer gave me a real grilling about my research on the McCloskys. I think things are starting to happen, Aggie. I'm being looked over!"

Tossing down her bag, Sophie did a triumphant jig in the middle of the carpet. Agnes abandoned the blouse to give Sophie a hug of congratulation. Then she stood back critically.

"They've been looking you over for weeks. It's something more."

"Oh . . . and I'm going out to dinner tonight. With Claude!"

The jig stopped. Sophie could see the wheels beginning to whir inside her friend's head.

"Dinner! Well why didn't you say so! Imagine! An actual date with the magnificent Claude!"

"Still part of the reimbursement deal. He might hold me up for ransom or fling me into debtor's prison if I refuse," Sophie returned with mournful and complete insincerity.

"Oh you poor thing! Forced at gunpoint like that! Where is he taking you?"

"Mallory's."

Agnes dropped her droll face in genuine astonishment.

"That posh place? Cripes! What are you going to wear?"

Sophie hadn't given a thought to this, and panic instantly ensued. Simultaneously, both women dived into their closets and it was a testament to their collective ingenuity that, in the bare hour and a half before Claude was to arrive, they turned Sophie out fit for an ambassador's reception. She wore a velvet dress of such a rich dark chocolate that light played off it as off the pelt of a live sable. Agnes contributed her garnet necklace and earrings, prized heirlooms from her grandmother, and the beaded evening bag she kept as a wall ornament. The matching garnet brooch they pinned on a velvet hair clip, and used it to tuck Sophie's hair back elegantly on one side. Without time to agonize disastrously over makeup choices, they dashed an impressionistic glow onto Sophie's face that looked positively inspired. A cream lace shawl, formerly a hand-worked tablecloth, completed the production.

"Wonderful," Agnes crowed. "Couldn't have done better if we'd worked on you for a week!

"You think so? My hair isn't going all wispy is it?"

"Wispy is in for evening. You'll floor him. You really will!"

"I'm not out to floor anybody. This is just practice for when I work undercover at political fund-raisers and such."

"Right," Agnes agreed. "And you just happen to adore looking at yourself in the mirror!"

Sophie grinned back. "Might as well enjoy it while I can."

She was pleased with her image. Much frothier than the clean-edged look she usually strove for, and pretty darn good for short notice. Fancy enough for Mallory's. And, said a hitherto unknown voice of vanity inside her, striking enough to show Claude what she could do if she set her mind to it.

Agnes dashed to her own room and returned with a perfume atomizer with which she proceeded to irrigate Sophie.

"It was my Christmas present, and it costs eighty dollars an ounce, so don't try to wipe it off on your palms like that."

"Agnes!" Sophie cried in aggravation, "I smell like a harem. Let's not give the guy ideas!"

"Let's give him all the ideas we can! You smell divine and you look good enough to compete with the food even in Mallory's. For heaven's sake, just go out and have fun!"

"After my past history with Claude, who knows how the evening will turn out," Sophie declared darkly, admiring the garnets nevertheless. "And why were you ironing your good blouse when I came in? Isn't tonight your night to wash the . . ."

The doorbell cut off the rest, and Sophie felt her stomach do a double flip, possessed by the same sweeping thrill one gets setting out on some new, completely unknown journey.

Stop it, stop it right now! she muttered inwardly. This is just a research trip. Someday you too might have to actually know something about food. She couldn't imagine why, though. Politics, scandal, war, and pestilence, that was her beat. She already knew everything she'd ever need to know about food.

Opening the door, she was rendered speechless at Claude, resplendent in bow tie and tux. Just the sight of him immobilized her for a moment as breath struggled and her knees felt wobbly. A purely physical effect, caused by electrical discharges, or static given off by his clothes. Just how much glorious maleness could a girl take on short notice at the door!

"C . . . come in," she managed, and he stepped into the apartment which, thank heaven, Agnes had just sped around making halfway presentable. The scent of pine came with him, and a supple animal grace that caused even Agnes to pause.

The impression of neatness was short-lived, for Nellie twined herself around Claude's ankles, leaving a trail of orange cat hair on the impeccable black purity. Sophie dived for the cat and managed to slam the coffee table in the process.

"Well," Claude commented genially, "I see we're off to our usual start. Let's hope we get through the rest of the evening in one piece. Shall we go?"

A muscle in his cheek quivered as Sophie approached, and she knew it was Agnes's perfume drifting about her in an expensive cloud. His gaze slid over the velvet of the dress and his head bent forward in approval.

"Like the outfit?" Sophie couldn't help asking.

"I certainly do," he returned, as he ushered her to the door. "I was afraid you might have been serious about the bells."

pleasure in all directions, and making no attempt to stop the unfurling. Not even bothered when she spotted a tuft of orange cat hair on Claude's left cuff, she reached lightly to brush it away.

"Nellie is always getting into trouble—like her name-sake."

"And who might that be?" Claude inquired, looking at Sophie's slender fingers on his wrist.

"The lady we named her after. Nellie McClung."

Claude committed the sin of putting his elbow on the table.

"You're not going to catch me on that one. I do know something about history."

"Nellie was my absolute heroine when I was ten," Sophie sighed, remembering when she had discovered this fiesty reformer. "That was my dramatic stage. I even held a mock parliament, the way Nellie did, to argue whether or not men should get the vote."

Why did Claude make her think he could actually see her striding up and down, haranguing her pint-size audience with the headlong passion she could, even then, so quickly summon.

"And what did you decide?"

"Oh we gave the poor dears the franchise—provided they didn't fill their heads with a lot of political nonsense and forget about their main job as breadwinners."

Speeding back along the paths of childhood, Sophie looked more girlish than Claude had ever seen her. Then her face settled into more serious lines.

"I wish the world would stick to more of Nellie's dictums."

"Like what?"

"Oh, like her idea of the Good Samaritan. According to Nellie, a real Good Samaritan picks up victims of crime from the wayside only so many times. After a while, he gets his friends, and cleans up the road!"

"And you know several roads that ought to be cleaned up?"

Chapter Five

"Yiiiii!"

Sophie screeched as the repaired Porsche took off in a roar that flung her back into the seat and kept her there as Claude booted up the twistiest streets he could find, barely braking at corners, leaping away from stop signs as though they scarcely existed. An age and a heart attack later, they decelerated as abruptly, and bucked to a halt in front of the restaurant. Under Claude's shameless grin, Sophie was decanted onto the sidewalk.

"I've been waiting a long time to do that." He slipped the keys, jingling, into his pocket. "Enjoyed every shriek."

Fair enough, Sophie thought grimly, but you just watch me take a cab home! She gathered her dignity in time to make an entrance—and promptly forgot her fright when the interior of Mallory's burst upon her with a splendor beyond even that which legend ascribed. Sharp pleasure welled in her that Claude should bring her to such a place—and volunteer to pay for it too!

To top it off, Claude had reserved the most secluded booth, a bowerlike corner with tea roses spreading their scent and a candle under Tiffany glass. Everything, from the riotous grape-and-vine wallpaper to the frosted sconces shaped like seashells and the ceiling frieze of nymphs and fauns, projected a frankly decadent, turn-of-the-century flavor Sophie found entrancing.

"I feel I ought to be wearing a naughty little tiara and ostrich feathers, at least. Is there some reason you picked

Mallory's?'' Sophie inquired, sliding almost next to Claude on the intimate, semicircular seat.

''Setting! Here, you belong to Paris—and the Belle Epoque!''

In the space of a millisecond, those green eyes made Sophie intensely aware of the velvet-clad curves of her own body against the plush seat, the dark paneling behind, the slender fronds of a palm rising tremulously from its hammered brass urn. Before she could even look to see if he were teasing, another century claimed her. They might have stepped from a carriage to take late supper after the opera, or met to tryst over smoked salmon and champagne. Before a flush got truly started, Sophie managed to brush the impression away. Besides, Claude now leaned back with a small, exasperating half smile.

''Actually, the chef here was on my Olympic team. I haven't had time yet to see how he's doing.''

''I see.'' No amount of ulterior motive could deflate Sophie. ''Does he know you're here?''

''Good lord, no! The trick is to check everything out long before he even suspects.''

Sophie beamed, thoroughly approving of such deviousness. After scanning the scene with an acutely practiced eye, Claude began to read from the ornate menu, investing the French with a sensuous roundness of tone Sophie had never suspected of the language. His descriptions were completely lost upon Sophie, who let the syllables wash over her and thought Claude the only man she knew who grew more charming when he turned pedantic.

A waiter appeared. At once, Claude embarked into a discussion, also in French, which involved elaborate gestures, intense exchanges, and many weighty pauses for consideration.

''What was that about?'' Sophie laughed when the man left. ''Did you decide the fate of the United Nations for another year?''

''I was merely ordering. The advice of a good waiter is invaluable. We'll be having his recommendations. Washed

down by a roguish little sauvignon, of course!'' he added merrily, in an unexpected parody of all the serious palaver of a moment before.

The atmosphere worked its magic, making Sophie feel pampered to an outrageous degree. Relax and enjoy, she told herself gleefully. Who knows when you'll ever get inside here again. Or get to bump knees with a fellow as toothsome as Claude Lacomte!

And oh how Claude fitted in, Sophie thought. With his fine head outlined against the polished wainscotting and candlelight flickering across his snowy shirt front, he might have been a young *vicomte* wintering in the capital, or an officer of the Queen's Hussars just out of uniform and determined to plunge into all the hedonistic delights military exercise had denied him.

''A penny for your thoughts.''

''Oh!'' Sophie whisked back to reality, fully aware she'd been caught staring at Claude's profile. ''It'll take more than a penny. Inflation, you know!''

Claude laughed, a little too knowingly. However, Sophi knew he'd also been eyeing the garnets nestled warmly the base of her throat, so they were even. A tiny spark de inside her dared to ignite and flame.

When the waiter returned, it was not with the allege saucy little sauvignon. Instead, he produced a bottle champagne—pink champagne—in an elaborate chased ver bucket. Claude looked nonplussed.

''This isn't what I ordered. You must have the table.''

The waiter only smiled. ''No, sir. Positively not!

Then the man was gone. Claude spread his han a chuckle. ''My dear friend Murray has discove presence. What we get for our dinner is anybody's

''Well, I approve of this soup,'' Sophie decla pling the delicate pale pink soup that had appea her in what looked like a real seashell. ''Yum!''

Whatever it was, it was exploding in bursts all over her tongue. But then, Sophie was exp

"You bet! Political back-scratching, profiteering developers, brainless polluters, people who have their cats declawed! As they say in *The Mikado*, 'I've got a little list!' "

She found she had polished off the soup while Claude took thoughtful sips from his glass. His eyes gleamed with the same look he had worn in Rita's—fascination in spite of himself.

"Do I see a crusader?" he asked, watching the sparks glinting under her lashes.

"Incurable. That's why I love the news. A person can make a real difference there—a person who digs out the facts and isn't afraid to lay them baldly out, that is!"

Before she knew it, Sophie had favored Claude with a ringing defense of the press as guardians of democracy. Only when her bracelet winged the fine crystal water goblet did she realize she was about to thump the table to emphasize her point.

"Sorry," she apologized sheepishly. "I get carried away."

"You don't say!" The double dimples appeared, their irony tempered by something undefinable. "You mean that under that hard-bitten exterior shines a genuine, gold-plated idealist?"

For just a fraction, Sophie hesitated. She took great pains to hide this part of herself in the often cynical newsroom. But Claude was not laughing at her. His eyes were only reckless—and inviting the same. She pulled a comic face.

"Drat! Caught out cold!"

"Oh, never cold," Claude murmured, his gaze playing over the soft curve of Sophie's cheek.

Sophie had to swallow quickly and fight not to look away. The glowing thing inside her flared, responding all by itself to a Claude who was not acting in the least like an impersonal coworker. To cover, she started talking about the power of the press again. And found herself still talking, twenty minutes later, when her soup bowl was spirited away. To her surprise, she discovered she'd been having a serious conversation with Claude—and having it so easily she hadn't even realized what an intense and profound exchange had been going on.

Why, I like him! she thought, taken with this entirely new aspect of the man. And she liked him in a way that had nothing to do with double dimples and that ravishingly unruly shock of hair loose at his forehead. Sophie, who had such forceful opinions on the world, knew from sad experience how hard it was to find a person she could really talk to.

In a minute, we're going to be exchanging book lists, she grinned inwardly. Mulling over the discovery of an intriguing intellect inside this already scrumptious man, Sophie sampled the next offering, which consisted of three perfect asparagus spears dashing through a brilliant center of orange vinaigrette sauce. For a flash, just a flash, the spoonful of the sauce took the outline of a heart, with the asparagus as arrows through it.

She looked again, but the picture didn't vanish until she disturbed the arrangement with her fork. When the pattern was gone, she smiled at her own foolishness. It had to be the wine, of course, already having its subtle effects. A lovely warmth, for instance, was drifting through her. At the same time, her senses sharpened, making her more and more intensely aware of Claude's body moving inside his jacket, of the light glancing off his hair, of the hand touching the cool clarity of the wineglass.

The waiter glided about them, so unobtrusive as to be almost invisible. Now Sophie knew why people came to Mallory's and gladly paid the astronomical prices. She felt cossetted, private, special beyond anything in her previous experience.

The gilded ambience was certainly doing its job. Doing it so well, in fact, that Sophie rapidly lost interest in freedom of speech in favor of watching the articulations of Claude's wrist where his cuff revealed the buffed gold of his watchband.

"So how did you happen to become a chef?" Sophie

Chapter Five

"Yiiiii!"

Sophie screeched as the repaired Porsche took off in a
roar that flung her back into the seat and kept her there as
Claude booted up the twistiest streets he could find, barely
braking at corners, leaping away from stop signs as though
they scarcely existed. An age and a heart attack later, they
decelerated as abruptly, and bucked to a halt in front of the
restaurant. Under Claude's shameless grin, Sophie was decanted onto the sidewalk.

"I've been waiting a long time to do that." He slipped
the keys, jingling, into his pocket. "Enjoyed every shriek."

Fair enough, Sophie thought grimly, but you just watch
me take a cab home! She gathered her dignity in time to
make an entrance—and promptly forgot her fright when
the interior of Mallory's burst upon her with a splendor
beyond even that which legend ascribed. Sharp pleasure
welled in her that Claude should bring her to such a place—
and volunteer to pay for it too!

To top it off, Claude had reserved the most secluded
booth, a bowerlike corner with tea roses spreading their
scent and a candle under Tiffany glass. Everything, from
the riotous grape-and-vine wallpaper to the frosted sconces
shaped like seashells and the ceiling frieze of nymphs and
fauns, projected a frankly decadent, turn-of-the-century flavor Sophie found entrancing.

"I feel I ought to be wearing a naughty little tiara and
ostrich feathers, at least. Is there some reason you picked

Mallory's?'' Sophie inquired, sliding almost next to Claude
on the intimate, semicircular seat.

"Setting! Here, you belong to Paris—and the Belle
Epoque!''

In the space of a millisecond, those green eyes made
Sophie intensely aware of the velvet-clad curves of her own
body against the plush seat, the dark paneling behind, the
slender fronds of a palm rising tremulously from its hammered brass urn. Before she could even look to see if he
were teasing, another century claimed her. They might have
stepped from a carriage to take late supper after the opera,
or met to tryst over smoked salmon and champagne. Before
a flush got truly started, Sophie managed to brush the impression away. Besides, Claude now leaned back with a
small, exasperating half smile.

"Actually, the chef here was on my Olympic team. I
haven't had time yet to see how he's doing.''

"I see.'' No amount of ulterior motive could deflate
Sophie. "Does he know you're here?''

"Good lord, no! The trick is to check everything out
long before he even suspects.''

Sophie beamed, thoroughly approving of such deviousness. After scanning the scene with an acutely practiced
eye, Claude began to read from the ornate menu, investing
the French with a sensuous roundness of tone Sophie had
never suspected of the language. His descriptions were
completely lost upon Sophie, who let the syllables wash
over her and thought Claude the only man she knew who
grew more charming when he turned pedantic.

A waiter appeared. At once, Claude embarked into a discussion, also in French, which involved elaborate gestures,
intense exchanges, and many weighty pauses for consideration.

"What was that about?'' Sophie laughed when the man
left. "Did you decide the fate of the United Nations for
another year?''

"I was merely ordering. The advice of a good waiter is
invaluable. We'll be having his recommendations. Washed

down by a roguish little sauvignon, of course!'' he added merrily, in an unexpected parody of all the serious palaver of a moment before.

The atmosphere worked its magic, making Sophie feel pampered to an outrageous degree. Relax and enjoy, she told herself gleefully. Who knows when you'll ever get inside here again. Or get to bump knees with a fellow as toothsome as Claude Lacomte!

And oh how Claude fitted in, Sophie thought. With his fine head outlined against the polished wainscotting and candlelight flickering across his snowy shirt front, he might have been a young *vicomte* wintering in the capital, or an officer of the Queen's Hussars just out of uniform and determined to plunge into all the hedonistic delights military exercise had denied him.

''A penny for your thoughts.''

''Oh!'' Sophie whisked back to reality, fully aware she'd been caught staring at Claude's profile. ''It'll take more than a penny. Inflation, you know!''

Claude laughed, a little too knowingly. However, Sophie knew he'd also been eyeing the garnets nestled warmly at the base of her throat, so they were even. A tiny spark deep inside her dared to ignite and flame.

When the waiter returned, it was not with the allegedly saucy little sauvignon. Instead, he produced a bottle of champagne—pink champagne—in an elaborate chased silver bucket. Claude looked nonplussed.

''This isn't what I ordered. You must have the wrong table.''

The waiter only smiled. ''No, sir. Positively not!''

Then the man was gone. Claude spread his hands with a chuckle. ''My dear friend Murray has discovered our presence. What we get for our dinner is anybody's guess.''

''Well, I approve of this soup,'' Sophie declared, sampling the delicate pale pink soup that had appeared before her in what looked like a real seashell. ''Yum!''

Whatever it was, it was exploding in bursts of delight all over her tongue. But then, Sophie was expanding with

pleasure in all directions, and making no attempt to stop
the unfurling. Not even bothered when she spotted a tuft
of orange cat hair on Claude's left cuff, she reached lightly
to brush it away.

"Nellie is always getting into trouble—like her name-
sake."

"And who might that be?" Claude inquired, looking at
Sophie's slender fingers on his wrist.

"The lady we named her after. Nellie McClung."

Claude committed the sin of putting his elbow on the
table.

"You're not going to catch me on that one. I do know
something about history."

"Nellie was my absolute heroine when I was ten,"
Sophie sighed, remembering when she had discovered this
fiesty reformer. "That was my dramatic stage. I even held
a mock parliament, the way Nellie did, to argue whether
or not men should get the vote."

Why did Claude make her think he could actually see
her striding up and down, haranguing her pint-size audience
with the headlong passion she could, even then, so quickly
summon.

"And what did you decide?"

"Oh we gave the poor dears the franchise—provided
they didn't fill their heads with a lot of political nonsense
and forget about their main job as breadwinners."

Speeding back along the paths of childhood, Sophie
looked more girlish than Claude had ever seen her. Then
her face settled into more serious lines.

"I wish the world would stick to more of Nellie's dictums."

"Like what?"

"Oh, like her idea of the Good Samaritan. According to
Nellie, a real Good Samaritan picks up victims of crime
from the wayside only so many times. After a while, he
gets his friends, and cleans up the road!"

"And you know several roads that ought to be cleaned
up?"

"You bet! Political back-scratching, profiteering developers, brainless polluters, people who have their cats declawed! As they say in *The Mikado*, 'I've got a little list!' "

She found she had polished off the soup while Claude took thoughtful sips from his glass. His eyes gleamed with the same look he had worn in Rita's—fascination in spite of himself.

"Do I see a crusader?" he asked, watching the sparks glinting under her lashes.

"Incurable. That's why I love the news. A person can make a real difference there—a person who digs out the facts and isn't afraid to lay them baldly out, that is!"

Before she knew it, Sophie had favored Claude with a ringing defense of the press as guardians of democracy. Only when her bracelet winged the fine crystal water goblet did she realize she was about to thump the table to emphasize her point.

"Sorry," she apologized sheepishly. "I get carried away."

"You don't say!" The double dimples appeared, their irony tempered by something undefinable. "You mean that under that hard-bitten exterior shines a genuine, gold-plated idealist?"

For just a fraction, Sophie hesitated. She took great pains to hide this part of herself in the often cynical newsroom. But Claude was not laughing at her. His eyes were only reckless—and inviting the same. She pulled a comic face.

"Drat! Caught out cold!"

"Oh, never cold," Claude murmured, his gaze playing over the soft curve of Sophie's cheek.

Sophie had to swallow quickly and fight not to look away. The glowing thing inside her flared, responding all by itself to a Claude who was not acting in the least like an impersonal coworker. To cover, she started talking about the power of the press again. And found herself still talking, twenty minutes later, when her soup bowl was spirited away. To her surprise, she discovered she'd been having a

serious conversation with Claude—and having it so easily
she hadn't even realized what an intense and profound
exchange had been going on.

Why, I like him! she thought, taken with this entirely new
aspect of the man. And she liked him in a way that had
nothing to do with double dimples and that ravishingly unruly shock of hair loose at his forehead. Sophie, who had
such forceful opinions on the world, knew from sad experience how hard it was to find a person she could really
talk to.

In a minute, we're going to be exchanging book lists,
she grinned inwardly. Mulling over the discovery of an
intriguing intellect inside this already scrumptious man,
Sophie sampled the next offering, which consisted of three
perfect asparagus spears dashing through a brilliant center
of orange vinaigrette sauce. For a flash, just a flash, the
spoonful of the sauce took the outline of a heart, with the
asparagus as arrows through it.

She looked again, but the picture didn't vanish until she
disturbed the arrangement with her fork. When the pattern
was gone, she smiled at her own foolishness. It had to be
the wine, of course, already having its subtle effects. A
lovely warmth, for instance, was drifting through her. At
the same time, her senses sharpened, making her more and
more intensely aware of Claude's body moving inside his
jacket, of the light glancing off his hair, of the hand touching the cool clarity of the wineglass.

The waiter glided about them, so unobtrusive as to be
almost invisible. Now Sophie knew why people came to
Mallory's and gladly paid the astronomical prices. She felt
cossetted, private, special beyond anything in her previous
experience.

The gilded ambience was certainly doing its job. Doing
it so well, in fact, that Sophie rapidly lost interest in freedom of speech in favor of watching the articulations of
Claude's wrist where his cuff revealed the buffed gold of
his watchband.

"So how did you happen to become a chef?" Sophie

asked, knowing that if the champagne were also at work on Claude, she could probably winkle all sorts of personal information out of him. The more time she spent with him, the hungrier she seemed to become for every little detail.

"On a bet with my sister!" And, at Sophie's astonished look, Claude laughed aloud. "She bet I couldn't get on the Olympic team, I bet I could. Remember, we grew up in the hotel business. We had to learn everything about it—including how to hold our own in the kitchen. I had to do my stint as executive chef before I took over full management. I won the bet," Claude's teeth gleamed, "but, of course, my sister got the hotel."

"You don't want to go back?"

"She loves running it. I'm happy to be the silent partner."

Sighing at the blissful taste, Sophie finished the final asparagus spear. The companionable Claude across from her seemed so far from the madman in the Porsche and the enraged one at the fire that Sophie had trouble believing the others existed.

"Funny, we have that in common. Your sister loves the hotel, my brother loves the hardware store. Yet the two of us, we . . ."

"We what?"

"We're restless types. Couldn't stay home if they paid us!"

She expected Claude to laugh. He only regarded her levelly.

"You said that. Not me."

Some challenge in the set of his jaw provoked Sophie and she opened her mouth to debate. Just then the entrée arrived, carried in with great pomp by their waiter and followed by, of all things, a violinist playing Rachmaninoff as he advanced.

Awed, Sophie watched as the waiter swept the dish from its silver serving salver and set it on the rich linen tablecloth. Everyone in the restaurant saw the ceremony and grew silent under the haunting strains of the violin. The waiter left with a bow but the violinist remained, stepping behind a knot of feathery palms so that his music drifted out, eerily disembodied, filling the air like a fine, invisible essence of romance.

"What is it?" Sophie asked in a hushed voice, inhaling the musky, savory smell unlike any she had ever experienced.

"Truffled breast of quail in wild rice," Claude returned, in a voice so oddly noted that Sophie peered at him keenly. He had the strangest expression on his face and had dropped into such a long silence that Sophie couldn't stand the suspense.

"What?" she demanded, but all the answer she got was Claude's face crinkling into an impenetrable smile.

"Eat up, enjoy. Believe me, now isn't the time for questions."

Shrugging slightly, Sophie began on the artful concoction, which demanded her full attention. After a moment, she managed some inconsequential chat, but a glance at Claude told her they both knew it was only a sham. With the arrival of the food and the music something had changed—and changed rather drastically. Underneath the words, the casual gestures, Sophie could feel a tension building up, a fine humming along the nerves as palpable and galvanizing as the static electricity in the air before seemingly calm weather breaks gloriously into a passionate storm.

Yet Claude was right. Her questions simply drowned in the exquisite taste, the lilting melody flowing around, the feel of the heavy linen napkin edged with cream lace. The meal had developed a mysterious significance Sophie couldn't penetrate. She only knew some kind of theater was going on, theater conducted with the restraint, the subtlety, the elegance of a saraband.

Through it all, Sophie kept expecting Claude to break into a lecture on gastronomy. However, he said not a word about it and ate as naturally as though he were at his own dining table. Yet all the while, Sophie knew he was watching her intently.

His attention blended into and became the essential part of the enchanting atmosphere woven about them by the great urns spilling over with flowers, the half-invisible staff, the music that would have melted glacial ice. There was certainly no ice in Sophie's veins. The champagne seemed to have filled them with a fine, crystalline pleasure which resonated with the melody and made her even more alive with awareness of Claude as a physical being. Or, to put it specifically, as a man!

After a while, she forgot to think, surrendering herself to the languid delights stealing over her. Were the lights growing rosier, she wondered, or was it just the wine she had drunk? And she noticed several couples glancing their way with that indulgent, pleased look people reserve for lovers.

Lovers, she thought, moving directly into the fantasy. They thought Claude was her lover. A week or two ago she might have laughed. Now, she tried the idea out, her breath soft, her mind imagining herself and Claude as others must see them—a handsome couple enveloped in an intimate glow.

"Oh!" Sophie crunched on something leathery and, in surprise, found a large bay leaf. Claude had a similar one lying on the edge of his plate.

"Somebody forgot to take the seasoning out," she grinned.

Claude raised one slow brow. "I don't think so."

"They left this in deliberately? Somebody could choke."

"Depends on who finds the leaf!"

He was looking odd again. Sophie put down her fork.

"It means something, doesn't it?"

One corner of Claude's mouth pulled down, but he remained silent. This was altogether too much for his companion.

"Out with it. What's with the bay leaves?"

"You really want to know?"

"I'm not giving up till I do!"

Claude paused as though considering the alternatives and finding none. Meaning, mischief, and some irrepressible intensity crept into his look.

"Very well. It's symbolism. According to legend, if you find a bay leaf in your food, you are in love!"

For a moment, Sophie forgot where she was, forgot everything except that she suddenly seemed to be falling and falling into the jade depths of his eyes. When she came to herself, she discovered she was on fire. To her amazement, she was blushing, a deep, pounding scarlet blush that started at her heels and worked upward into every pore of her body. She who struggled so hard to be hard-boiled, fought with the surging heat and finally, at long last, suppressed the storm.

Sophie sat staring at Claude. Gradually, what had been odd began to penetrate. Everything served up, including the violinist, had been designed . . . surely not deliberately . . . to be shamelessly romantic. Claude's eyes were dancing.

"I see by your look," he murmured, "that it's beginning to dawn that there is something unique about his meal."

"What?" Sophie asked, not at all sure, after her frantic attack of blushing, she really wanted to know.

"It's Murray's Valentine special. He's trying it out on us."

"Valentine! But it's June!"

Claude flung a lean hand through the air.

"My dear, it might take him another three months to perfect it. Then he has to assure consistent production by the staff. Then he has to see the ingredients will be available in February and put in his order early enough to secure the very best. Then word must go out to favored patrons so that they can be sure to make their reservations soon enough to assure a table. And then . . ."

"Okay, okay," Sophie laughed, "I get the picture. Who would have guessed the effort in one fancy dinner." She paused, but inquisitiveness bested her. "What does the rest of it mean?"

"The soup came in the seashell of Venus, born of the sea, the asparagus spears darting into the heart speak for themselves, truffles are so rare they are kept in safes and served only to the most precious of people . . . shall I go on?"

Though he was smiling his familiar smile, the husky vibration in his voice gripped Sophie as he spoke. For all that she tried to suppress it, she knew she had sent him a fiery signal with her blush, and nothing now could negate it. Claude sat close enough now so that Sophie's leg brushed the fabric of his trousers, the soft scrape sending a quiver along her calf. With deliberate ease, Claude slipped his hand over hers on the table. The warmth and the contact, taking Sophie by surprise, made her quietly gasp.

"You know," he murmured, his eyes crinkling at the corners, "you are looking less and less hard-boiled by the minute."

Sophie's mouth opened slightly, but to no avail, for she found herself speechless. She seemed to have fallen into some magical space which caused the room round her to become faintly misted, softly out of focus. At the same time, the sway of the violin made her feel she was flying.

You are falling for the guy, announced a voice inside her head. Claude Lacomte is making his move and you are toppling like a ninepin!

His thumb brushed the inside of Sophie's palm thrillingly even as the voice started to argue—though who the voice was arguing with, Sophie couldn't have said. She herself knew very well that she ought to pull her hand away and sit on it if she had to. When people such as Claude got into gear, they could stun an elephant with simple raw charisma. She ought to know better. She had sworn never to get into this kind of mess again.

Perversely, the moment Sophie showed signs of regaining shreds of rationality, the voice took up the other side.

Oh go ahead, it whispered. It's your night out. You can handle it this once. You're awash in champagne, dressed to kill, and you've just eaten truffled quail. Take a chance and enjoy!

Logic gasped once and sank without a trace.

When Sophie didn't withdraw her hand, everything changed, including Claude. The irony vanished, and a heady masculine warmth radiated outward. Sophie felt the shift—and a crazy, half-apprehensive flutter caught at her midriff. What if the pleasant fantasy got out of bounds? What if it actually turned real!

The arrival of dessert, amidst discreet and elegant fanfare, saved Sophie from trying to think about this. The dessert was also amazing—tiny plump pears marinated in brandy, dipped in chocoate, and drenched with something that glimmered like rubies. The candle flared. Claude's face leaped into a vivid light for a moment in the golden flame. His eyes caught Sophie's and gleamed with a jubilant message that set Sophie's blood racing.

"It's . . . wonderful!" she breathed, telling herself she meant the dessert. She twisted to thank the waiter for his skill. As she did so, she caught a glimpse of the booth next to their own. The partial outline of a face arrested her. She craned her neck—then froze in the middle of a breath.

Ellis Hooper! Of the lately incinerated Hooper Developments—engaged in conversation with another man. Though Sophie couldn't see the other man clearly, she knew at once that he was of the silk-suited, shifty-eyed, unsavory variety.

Instantly, Sophie's powerful news instinct kicked to life, overriding even the dizzying effects of Claude's nearness. Collusion, it screamed. No honest developer would have dinner with a man as sleazy-looking as that! As Hooper spoke in a low, intense manner. Sophie felt the nerves at her nape prickle and her ears hum. She just *had* to find out what was going on.

Claude turned her hand over, cupped it with his own, then brushed it ever so lightly with his lips. Sophie, by sheer will, managed to remain motionless. Claude frowned slightly.

"Why," he asked, after a moment, "does such a red-blooded creature as yourself give off such strong 'I'm busy' signals? Is it something in your past?"

"My past?"

Sophie opened her eyes as if in surprise. She had to keep her head toward Claude so that Hooper wouldn't see her interest. And, on top of everything, she was trying to keep a lid on her pulse rate. Claude smiled, showing all his magnificent teeth.

"Come on. You inveigled my status out of me within a half hour of meeting me. Your turn now."

Sophie sensed Hooper nodding brusquely. "Perhaps," was all she could think of to say, now torn between Claude and the next booth. Claude's thumb caressed her palm. She didn't even have the sense, she thought, to tease him back. Dangerous, dangerous!

"Perhaps what?"

Stan Winterly rampaged back through memory. Sophie shook her head. "It's too silly." Hooper's companion was grunting morosely and Sophie was dying to know over what.

"Concerning you, nothing could possibly be too silly."

He was smiling, but so intimately Sophie almost forgot about Hooper. Tenaciously, she fought Claude's pull, but a delighted giggle burst from her anyway. Hooper glanced round before she had a chance to smother it.

"Diplomacy isn't exactly your strong suit either," she couldn't resist saying. "Suppose you tell me about the string of lovelies you left behind in Montreal."

Amazingly, she was flirting. Even as the joy of it beat high in Sophie, she used the banter as cover to peep at Hooper. Above all, she mustn't change the mood or let Claude know who sat behind them lest he upset everything. Besides, she really did want to know about Marianne. Claude shook his head, laughing.

"I don't tell tales out of school!"

"And you expect me to spill everything about Stan . . . I mean, do the same!"

Claude lifted her other hand to his lips and laid a kiss in the palm. Sophie felt something lurch inside her and she half closed her eyes. Claude laid a second kiss, this time on the tender inside of her wrist.

"Ah, so now we have a name at least. Who was Stan?"

"Claude! People are looking!" The turbulence Claude was rousing touched Sophie with a prick of panic. Claude drew his thumb sensuously over the part of her wrist where the pulse leaped and veins showed under the white skin.

"I'd insult the meal if I hadn't kissed at least some part of you by now. Tell me about Stan or I'll never stop!"

He had progressed to the back of her hand and on to her wrist, sending butterfly flutters all the way to her elbow. At the same time, out of the corner of her eye, she saw Hooper frown and look urgent. She couldn't risk a fuss or Hooper's attention might be diverted again.

"I see," she murmured, managing to sound provocative. She shifted slightly, for a better angle on Hooper.

"Meet Tonelli Tuesday . . ." she heard Hooper say.

At Sophie's inviting tone, Claude looked even more pleased, and bent his head toward her. His answer, silky and warm, was nonetheless blotted out by Sophie's intense concentration on her quarry. She could pick out Hooper's voice and catch maddening fragments but could not make out what he was saying. From glimpsed expressions, she knew it was something serious, something she and the world ought to know.

Then Claude reached her elbow and his kisses pulled Sophie away from Hooper, away from everything save the honeyed seduction of his breath. "Oh!" she gasped at the wild tingles shooting along her nerve ends. How could such little kisses have such a dazzling effect!

Sophie dropped her head so that her hair screened her face. The wrinkled, stricken countenances of the McCloskys flashed into her mind, then another brush of Claude's lips obscured even that gripping image. She mustn't lose it. No, she mustn't. Not here. Not when she might have a chance to do something about their plight.

Oh it was maddening, maddening to have Hooper only feet away, separated by a bit of partition and a vase of flowers. It was too rare, too important an opportunity to be missed!

"Give up yet?" Claude was rumbling. "I won't necessarily stop at your shoulder, though such a delectable shoulder it is!"

Protected from view by the same grove of palms screening the violinist, Claude was now working on the smooth flesh of Sophie's upper arm. When he felt Sophie quiver involuntarily under his touch, he smiled; his eyes seemed to speak to her, telling of an evening made perfect by her presence.

Sophie closed her lashes in an attempt to shut out the intoxicating effect Claude was having. Claude took this for acquiescence and tucked her hand gently against his side. He failed to noticed her other hand slide into her evening bag which lay by the vase on the divider. She sought an object she never went anywhere without—a tiny spy camera which lay beside the equally tiny, high-powered tape recorder which had cost her a fortune and, until now, she had never had an opportunity to use.

Claude edged closer, his gaze fixed on the tempting places of Sophie's neck. The pine tang of his aftershave tantalized Sophie's nostrils, the candlelight touched a pulse along his jaw. Sophie leaned back, the camera in the palm of her hand. She had practiced with the buttons until she could use them in her sleep. Her movement seemed to yield her throat to Claude's caresses and Claude responded with a rumble deep in his chest.

"Could Stan," he husked out, "make you smile this way? If he could, and he left you, he was a block-headed fool."

"He . . . ah . . ."

Claude stopped her words with a kiss on the naked tip of her shoulder. Sophie's breath caught, and only by dint of great effort did she manage to keep some of her attention on the booth she was watching over Claude's shoulder. The man with Hooper now looked nervous. He didn't want to be there at all.

I have to get proof of his identity, Sophie thought. I have to establish where the meeting was and when.

Her hand closed tightly on the tiny camera and her heart began to pound. Claude said something else, but Sophie didn't catch it. Be cool, be cool, she told herself, caught up in a turmoil of conflicting pulls. You must do your job!

She murmured to Claude, unaware of what came out of her mouth, only that her voice was velvet, her lashes lowered. At all costs, Claude must not give the show away. She slipped the camera into the folds of the lace shawl pooled around her. Claude's face was so close she could feel his breath. Her head felt entirely full of bubbles while her heart began alternately to thud heavily and die away. If she could just manage to hold together to pull this off, Beirut would be no challenge at all!

Claude was now speaking to her in low, dusky tones, but the blood was rushing so madly in Sophie's ears that she could scarcely pick up a word. Hooper broke off conversation and frowned in her direction. She bent her head away.

"Yes?" she heard herself saying. "Really . . ."

Claude paused, looking at her a little oddly, but she favored him with such an enchanting smile that he went on again.

"I was saying that when a man finds a woman he . . ."

The rest was lost as Sophie saw Hooper suddenly down the remainder of his drink and signal for the bill. At once, his companion followed suit, scraping back his chair. Panic shot through Sophie. Her quarry was leaving. She had to do what she had to do—and still keep Claude from blowing the operation!

Madly, she looked around for something to cover her action—and lit upon the exquisite chocolate-dipped pears. Smiling in what she hoped was a wickedly enticing manner, she picked one up and seductively fed it to Claude—perhaps exactly what Murray had designed them for. In surprise and pleasure, he accepted the offering, easing still closer as though to taste Sophie's lips.

It took just about all Sophie's strength to not simply melt. The nearness of him was very heady, but just then Hooper was plunking down a wad of cash and looking toward the door. Swiftly, lightly, Sophie slipped an arm up to Claude's shoulder, drawing him round so that she had a clear line of view. Her other hand also came up, ostensibly to brush back the shawl. Under it, Sophie held the tiny camera, which she pointed at Hooper and his companion.

Turn, turn this way, she willed them—and turn they did. Claude's face came closer, his eyes on Sophie's mouth, his look soft, almost eager. Sophie brushed her free hand against his cheek, catching him up into a long, timeless moment—broken sharply by a series of tiny clicks!

Claude might have missed the clicks, but he certainly didn't miss the camera when the corner of the shawl caught under Sophie's elbow, jerking the item from Sophie's fingers so that it fell with a plunk to the seat. Claude stared at it as though a lizard had dropped from the ceiling.

"What the . . ."

At the same time, Hooper paused in the midst of slipping his wallet back into his pocket and peered yet again at Sophie's booth. Instantly, Sophie's arm slid the rest of the way round Claude's shoulders, the gesture of a woman at ease in a fine restaurant, warmed by champagne, now teasing her lover.

Only her fingers clamped onto Claude's neck, above his collar, with all the lightning ferocity of a cobra paralyzing a victim just before the kill.

"Freeze!"

Sophie hissed the command under cover of a smile so enormous, so luminous with adoration, that Claude was utterly immobilized—and remained so for the few moments it took for Hooper and his companion to vanish through the door.

Gingerly, very gingerly, Sophie released her grip. She felt Claude breathe once, fiercely, under his ribs. His look was so incredulous that Sophie might have laughed—had she been a far braver person, that is, and not totally rattled by what she had just done.

"That," Claude observed, "looks very like a camera."

"Yes. I . . . er, just took a picture."

Sophie began stuffing the camera into her bag, astonished to find her own heart thundering and her skin clammy and pale.

"A picture? Of what?"

He was so close that, for a fraction, Sophie couldn't remember what. Then her excitement returned like a fever.

"Ellis Hooper! You know. Of Hooper Developments. That fire we went to. He was just next to us. You should have seen the character he was talking to!"

Naturally, in her flurry, Sophie upset her handbag, spilling out not only the camera but the tiny tape recorder. Unbelieving shock spread across Claude's face.

"And that tape was running too!"

"Certainly not!" Sophie retorted. "It's highly illegal to tape conversation without permission, not to mention . . ."

"Then why are the reels turning?"

"They are not!"

She tried to snatch the machine, but Claude already had it in his hand, showing her the tape indeed turning inside. Yes, she had turned it on, with unconscious efficiency, when she had reached for the camera. In the midst of a second lunge, she realized that heads were turning and their heated words crackled in the restaurant's reverend hush. Claude released the machine abruptly and signaled for the check, his face a thundercloud.

"I think we better go before we create any more of a scene. We just have to thank the—"

Before Claude could finish, a stocky fellow in white appeared, beaming vastly. Curly hair poked from under his chef's hat and large ears gave him the air of a friendly retriever.

"Thought I wouldn't spot you, eh?" Murray chortled. "I knew as soon as you stepped in the door. Just the fellow to try out my lovebird special on. I've been sweating it up since morning, trying to get the presentation right. What I want to know is has it done the trick?''

Murray failed to notice that Claude's jaw was stiff as iron and that Sophie was still breathing hotly from her recent exchange. Cheeks flushed, she scrambled for something to say.

''What trick?''

Murray favored Sophie with a mighty wink.

''Why, make you two fall in love. We've been trying to get Claude married off for the last five years. The way he was looking at you when he came in the door, I thought perhaps my expenditure of truffles had a chance.''

Gleefully, Murray watched the dark flush climbing up Claude's neck. A flush whose origin he had completely mistaken.

He's going to explode again, Sophie thought in panic. Right here in front of all these people!

Emotions galloped through her like wild horses on the loose. All she could think of to do was slip her arm through Claude's as though it belonged there and turn on her best smile.

''Nobody,'' she assured Murray, ''could have made more progress in that direction than you.''

''Right!'' Claude added with biting irony only Sophie recognized. ''Progress indeed!''

They managed to thank Murray convincingly and escape.

''To think,'' Claude hissed under his breath when they were outside. ''I was actually getting romantic—with Mata Hari!''

Claude hustled her into the car and drove her, in shrieking silence, home, the Porsche eating up the streets voraciously. He didn't speak, not even when he ushered her out of the car and up to her own door—and Sophie didn't dare any more explaining. He took five steps toward the car—then turned back sharply.

''Wait a minute!'' he exploded, ''I owe it to Murray not to let that dinner go completely to waste!''

Before Sophie knew it, he was on the porch again and she was in his arms. His mouth claimed hers, kissing her with ferocious intentness. She was crushed against Claude's chest, seeing him for a moment, looming in the halo of the porchlight, then losing herself in the breathless, bewildering ecstasy visited upon her.

When Claude pulled his head away, he held her by the shoulders, staring down at her in the dim illumination, the shock of hair at his forehead loose and wild. Then he released her, turned on his heel and stalked back to the Porsche. Before Sophie could even get her breath back, the scarlet taillights had vanished into the night.

Chapter Six

That night, Sophie tumbled through a restless half consciousness, moaning softly as Claude's lips pressed hers as sensuously as though he had followed her into the room. Each time, Sophie came to with a start, struggling to remember where she was. Details of the dinner unrolled in her mind, shot through with violin music. Again and again, Claude's face approached in the gloom. Again and again, his tall figure turned on its heel and vanished into the night. Again and again, happiness and loss knotted themselves inextricably in her breast.

In the morning, Sophie woke slowly, dark smudges under her eyes and echoes of Rachmaninoff befuddling her mind. She forgot all about breakfast, and it wasn't until she got to work that she put her hand in her purse and encountered the tiny camera and tape recorder. She shot bolt upright.

Good grief! She'd actually forgotten her coup of the evening before! Not even Stan had addled her brain this badly. Blasted at last from her altered state, Sophie dug out her evidence. She must stop acting the mooncalf and get back on track at once.

The tiny film and tape restored Sophie to normal. As normal as possible, that is, while tearing into Greer's office in a state of high excitement and blurting out what she had and how she had gotten it. Greer rose up out of her chair.

"Spy photographs! Secret tapes! Hardly newsroom style, Sophie. I'll have to discuss it with Mr. Owen!"

Taking possession of both, Greer popped them grimly
into her desk drawer. Sophie felt her stomach plunge, afraid
there might be nothing on them but white noise, or
Claude's ear. Why oh why hadn't she checked before gal-
lumphing in like a pup who's found its first bone? Chas-
tened, Sophie retreated, only to discover Agnes, fingers
limp on her keyboard, gazing at the blank wall as dreamily
as if visions of sugarplums danced across the plaster.

"Hey, where were you when I got in last night?" Sophie
suddenly wanted to know. "And, as a matter of fact, where
were you this morning?"

She received only a languid sigh and a flutter of lashes
toward the weather desk. Sid lolled there, his latest printout
upside down, as hopelessly dazed as Agnes.

"Oh!" Sophie looked from one to the other, then said,
"OH!" much louder, as the penny dropped. She stared
hard at her friend who, for the first time in her life, seemed
completely uninterested in words.

Sliding into her own chair, Sophie felt queer inside.
Agnes had spent the night out with Sid and was over the
rainbow as a result. Over the rainbow in a way witty, ironic
Agnes had never been in any other romance she had in-
dulged in over the years.

Unable, quite, to grapple with this new reality, Sophie
tried to work. The harder she worked, the odder the pit of
her stomach felt. What if she were losing Agnes? What if
Agnes went off with a man for real? Where then would
Sophie be!

The loss of her best friend wasn't a possibility Sophie
had considered before. Not even when she dreamed of
dashing off as a foreign correspondent. Now she had the
distinct, uncomfortable feeling that life was shifting under
her feet. Shifting rudely, without warning—and there
wasn't a thing she could do about it.

Her own adventure returned to her—and Sophie doggedly fought the memory away. Claude's tempestuous kiss
was now mixed with the sharp echo of his footsteps as he

strode away. Her new sense of gaping holes and pitfalls made her loathe to admit how strongly she had fallen under his spell. All day she struggled against the sensation, waiting until after work, when she finally cornered Agnes in the bedroom.

"You," she declared, "had better tell me the details."

Agnes shucked out of her dress and into her jeans.

"We saw, we met, we're falling for each other. What's more to tell?"

"Lots more, from the look of you," Sophie said severely—and with more anxiety than she cared to admit.

Her answer was a bemused sigh—and a look implying whole new galaxies of worldly wisdom.

"You ought to try it yourself sometime."

"With whom?"

"The redoubtable Claude, of course. And you haven't told me about Mallory's."

Once, Sophie would have been dying to spill every detail of the elaborate, wickedly romantic dinner. But the theme of the dinner was all tangled up with Claude—and with feelings that gave Sophie a hot rush. She skipped through a breezy description of the decor and superb service. Then her eyes lit up.

"You'll never guess what happened. Remember Ellis Hooper?"

Making the most of the drama, Sophie related the saga of Hooper and her spy equipment. Agnes whistled, impressed, even though her head was inside the sweatshirt she was pulling on.

"Wow! What was on the tape?"

"Ah . . . I didn't get a chance to listen."

Agnes popped her head out of the neck hole.

"Didn't get a chance! You wouldn't miss seeing what you had if you had to fight off a horde of Huns and hang upside down like a bat while you did it!"

Sophie opened her mouth, but not even the most implausible of excuses would come out of it. Agnes snapped her fingers.

"Claude! I knew it! Now who's talking about involved!"

"Not involved, just . . . distracted. He wasn't happy about me snapping a picture past the side of his neck."

"Well, do tell!"

On the bed, Agnes crossed her legs like a sage while Sophie sketched the scrap that ended the evening, significantly omitting the nature of the Valentine dinner and the sizzling kiss which had really been responsible for her forgetful condition.

"Are you going to have to apologize again?"

"It had nothing to do with the station. Greer and the Buckeroo can't make me."

It was a stubborn, intransigent statement, but Sophie meant to stick to it—all the more because her own conscience plucked at her. Sophie was confused about Claude—and confusion brought out the fight in her, the bulldog tendency that was both her strongest asset and greatest liability, the tendency to take a stance, right or wrong, and hold it to the death.

Sighing, Agnes said nothing. When Sophie looked like that, it was futile to argue. Sophie was left to herself for the next few days, which were bad enough. She found herself staring at her work, unable to remember what she had been reading—or at the wall, acting exactly the way Agnes had been acting. Worse still, she felt the whisper of Claude's lips when she was supposed to be practicing with the editing machine. She couldn't go to bed without softly sliding into Claude's arms. Obsessively, she wondered what might have happened had she not derailed the evening with her investigative reporter routine.

Claude, she supposed, was probably still mad, for no rangy figure waylaid Sophie in the hall, no tasty offering appeared on the mail cart. He had been pouring on the romance while she used him as cover to stalk Hooper. How could the red-blooded male in him not be offended when, for all his grand effort, he hadn't even had her attention!

Little did he know!

Sophie licked dry lips and sighed. He'd had her attention all right. Had it to the extent that she now sometimes had difficulty remembering the alphabet. Gripped by a turmoil alien to her normal, energetic self, Sophie actually drooped at her desk. Drooped enough for Agnes to tackle her abruptly.

"Look, whatever happened between you and Claude, why don't you go down to Studio E and straighten it out. That'll clear the air until your next ruckus and I won't have to keep looking at that hound dog face across the room any more!"

Sophie made a fist around her pencil, hating to admit she was softening up about speaking to Claude. One part of her was dismayed at the swirl of badly timed, out-of-control feelings he had stirred up. The other part wanted to mindlessly, eagerly lollop down to Studio E simply to be in Claude's presence again. It was because of this last that Sophie had been resisting. She hated being told what to do—even by her own inner promptings.

Greer changed that when she emerged from her office and strode over to where Sophie was sorting unemployment statistics.

"That film and tape—the police have them. They just called to say they want to keep them. They seem quite interested."

Sophie gulped in an excited breath. The police might be using them to get the McCloskys off the hook!

Flushed with triumph, Sophie suddenly felt she could be friends with the entire world. Before she knew what she was doing, she was speeding through the halls, only realizing outside of Studio E how irresistible was the force pulling her in Claude's direction—and how hard she had been fighting it.

Oh well, she'd just tell him about the police. Yes, let him put that in his pipe and smoke it, after making all that fuss about a little journalistic initiative. A face-to-face chat was exactly the thing to squelch all the welter of feelings

clamoring inside her and put Claude firmly back into perspective!

She grinned as she went, pleased with how, even in the
newsroom, she had managed to keep her finger on the pulse
of Claude's show. Just the way she had checked out that
"little hotel" of Claude's on Rue St. Catherine, only to
discover it was one of the most select and elite establish-
ments in Montreal.

She found Studio E jammed by an audience just settling
in. She'd picked the worst of all moments to collar
Claude—right when he was getting ready to do a show.
On the other hand, she reasoned nimbly, Claude would
likely be so distracted he'd have to accept her news with
good grace and forgo, in front of his crew, any of the py-
rotechnics he was prone to.

As the last of the audience streamed by her, Sophie
picked up the buzz that made the atmosphere in the studio
so palpably electric. Every seat was taken, and a number
of people were willing to prop themselves against the walls.
The demographic breakdown was easy. The audience consisted of women, all gazing raptly at the spot on the set
where Claude would appear.

But I'm the one he's kissed!

The thought sprang up so unbidden that Sophie nearly
sprawled over an outstretched foot. She pushed the thought
away, mainly because it raised the awful question of who
else Claude had kissed. Most especially, if he had kissed
his lovely assistant, Marianne.

The set informed Sophie at a glance that her previous
impression of Claude, as an exacting perfectionist, was utterly true. His countertops were spotless, the utensils lined
up like an army ready for war, and the ingredients for today's program displayed with the flair of an impressionist
work of art.

Or was it all the doing of Marianne, who slaved while
Claude reaped the glory? Dampened, Sophie peered around
in search of the lady who, no doubt, did the gofering, or-

ganizing, and cleaning up afterward. Sophie knew all about being an assistant.

Time being short, Sophie sidled round to the back of the set, where she knew Claude would be getting ready. Sure enough, he loomed up, clad in intimidating white, looking prepared to minister to the Czar of all the Russias.

Sophie was unprepared for his impact. All she could think of, at first, was the breathtakingly sexy contrast between the warm, living, masculine skin and the icy crispness of his jacket. Her stomach contracted with swift longing. For all that she had vowed not to think about his kiss, it came back to her as though he had just that moment taken his mouth away. Oh to run forward and bury her face against the firm, inviting line of his jaw.

He was busy checking a clipboard with swift competence. A man who loved order, Sophie thought, trying to subdue the chaos in her breast. Who had his life under control. Who would have no patience with chaos—inside bosoms or elsewhere.

Unable to help herself, Sophie's gaze flew to his mouth, straight now in concentration, and suffered a frisson of remembered pleasure. She struggled to hang onto her perspective. Yes, she wanted to make peace, had to make peace, despite the sparks she and Claude struck off each other—and she shivered with involuntary anticipation of what such peace might lead to.

Fixing her face into studied calm, Sophie approached from behind. Almost instantly, Claude whirled, spotting her among the shifting swirls of people. Sophie's heart skittered even as little cords appeared along his throat and his eyes darkened with something hot and primal.

"Well, well. Another spectator?"

"How did you know I was here?"

"Same way I know a hurricane's due—by the hairs standing up on the back of my neck. I suppose you've come to watch?"

So, he was still seething from the escapade in the restaurant. Sophie's blood, stirred by the flash between them, threatened to rise. Firmly, she resisted.

"I haven't time. Besides, there's quite enough people out there willing to give a rave review."

"No doubt!" Claude quirked one brow. They both knew the audience was entirely of the female persuasion. Sophie clung hard to breezy nonchalance.

"Anyway, after our last conversation, I don't think a rave review from me would cut much ice."

Claude laughed outright, releasing the tension a little and mocking her infuriatingly with his double dimples.

"You're right. What would I do with a rave review from a woman who thinks omelettes boil."

Was he baiting her? Yes he was. Sophie felt her hackles rise and grew even more determined to make him appreciate her peacemaking mission.

"Look, I only have a moment, and came here to speak to you about the other night at Mallory's. That picture . . ."

"Gangway, all!"

Cliff, the studio handyman, lurched through shouldering a load of boards. Only then did Sophie notice that she and Claude were standing in a ring of tools next to a skeletal structure, some planned addition to the set, towering shakily. Skinny, indispensable, irreverent Cliff, winked at Claude as he passed.

"You'll get the new backdrop tomorrow morning, tops."

"Ten minutes, Claude," said the floor director speeding past. "It's packed to the rafters out there."

Studio activity washed in again as someone handed Claude another sheet for his clipboard and Vania, the makeup lady, tugged critically at his collar. Sophie stepped closer.

"Look, I came to explain about the camera and I'm not leaving till I do!"

That brought Claude around again, eyes snapping.

"Well well, so my opinion is that important, is it? I'm honored. I never would have . . ."

"Don't you dare patronize me!"

Thunderclouds swarmed into Claude's face. He shook Vania off.

"For your information, I never patronize people. Especially not a woman I've ... Watch out!"

At Claude's advance, Sophie stepped unthinkingly backward and wondered why Claude should suddenly try to grab her. His fingers closed on her arm just as her back slammed into a two-by-four. Naturally, this two-by-four propped up the half-built back drop. Everything went into horrified slow motion as the structure teetered, twisted, and crashed down—right on top of Claude! The last thing Sophie caught was Claude's look of astonishment as he vanished under the splintering heap of lumber. As frozen paralysis gripped the crew, Sophie sprang to life.

"Oh no!" she pulled at the heavy wood. "Are you hurt?"

Other hands tore the debris away to reveal Claude sprawled sideways, clutching at his arm and gritting his teeth in an effort to bite back furious groans.

"What does it look like!"

The rest of the crew stampeded over, including Martin Scorley, the producer, panic already clutching at his face.

"You're on in six minutes. You can't be hurt."

Claude's attempt to rise ended in a sharp, rasping grunt. His shoulder thudded to the floor again.

"My arm! I think she's broken my arm!"

Everything erupted into confusion and shouts for an ambulance. When the emergency people finally appeared, they did indeed pronounce Claude's wrist probably fractured and his leg iffy as well, though they were more positive about his spine. They plopped him onto a stretcher, strapped him down so that his protesting wriggles were useless. At the sight of Claude being hoisted onto the gurney, Martin Scorley leaped to block the way.

"You can't take him away! He's got a show to put on!"

The biggest attendant laughed.

"Not today, he doesn't. He's going straight to the fracture room. Better call in Mickey Rooney."

Martin paled, looking for a moment as though he might tear Claude from the stretcher himself. The chaotic retinue following the gurney over the obstacle course of cables toward the exit squeezed him aside. Overhead, the studio clock inexorably ticked away time and money and the Buckeroo's good temper, telling Martin he had to get something, anything, on tape. Martin lunged, grabbing Sophie out of the thick of the pack.

"Go out there," he pointed toward the set and the waiting audience. "Go out there and do Claude's show."

He said the one thing in the world that could take Sophie's mind off Claude's injuries. Her jaw unhinged and she stopped her struggle against the meaty paw gripping her shoulder.

"But I can't . . ."

"Sure you can. You're a woman, aren't you? Just make something out of the stuff out there. Scrambled eggs. Anything—so long as you get it on the stove and keep talking and keep the audience quiet. We'll worry about everything later."

Everything Sophie had ever heard about Martin flashed through her head—especially the way the jock producer rattled charts and let Claude have the run of things with no one out there in television land any the wiser. Martin, who would probably have been out of work but for the Buckeroo, was loathe to interfere. It proved a happy arrangement for both Martin and Claude—but not for Sophie, whose knees, in this moment of crisis and opportunity, treacherously turned to water.

"Marianne! Where's Marianne? She can do it!"

"Marianne's laid out with a virus. Flu or something."

Martin was now physically shoving Sophie toward the open dais. Visible beyond, the waiting spectators muttered restively, disturbed by the unseen flurry behind the scenes. Everyone knew that an audience, like any pack of hungry lions, had to be fed before they devoured alive the hapless unfortunate depriving them of a show. Seeing Sophie weaken, Martin grew more wily.

"It's you big chance, kid. Do well and you'll be noticed. You surely will!"

This lure was old as showbiz—and still as magic. The problem of the show being a cooking show vanished from Sophie's mind. What she saw was the cameras at the ready, the lights blazing, the people eager for action to begin. Her heart thudded even faster than it was already going and she felt her blood rushing to her head. Unfortunately Claude, whose stretcher was jammed at the door, overheard Martin and tried violently to sit up, unmindful of the stabs of pain ripping through him.

"No!" he bellowed furiously at the top of his lungs. "No, no! Not my show. Anybody but her!"

The sheer menace of the roar caused Sophie to spin. At any other time, the tone would have turned her livid, but she was still too shaken with guilt and anxiety over Claude's accident.

"Claude's hurt! I can't take advantage of . . ."

Martin clamped a second paw on Sophie's body. His battered, ex-prizefighter face crumpled into pathos and concern.

"But Claude can't do it. Claude needs you!" Martin's beagle eyes appealed to every noble sentiment Sophie possessed. "Do it for Claude!"

Do it for Claude!

Sophie looked toward the stretcher but Claude was invisible due to hands holding him down. Even as she stood, the stretcher jerked free, leaving Claude with a picture of Sophie immobile in Martin's clutches, stars glittering in her eyes and her impulse to follow the gurney dying in a flurry of golden promises.

When Martin saw that Sophie wasn't going to bolt, he released her, leaving open only the path that led toward the lights and the cameras. Her first step in that direction resulted from a sturdy thump on the shoulder blades.

"Wing it, sweetheart. You can do it."

A hundred trumpets sounded in Sophie's head, the clarion notes she had been waiting for all her life. She gulped, straightened, and summoned her resources. She had not studied for so many years to crumple when the call to action came. No matter if she could hardly boil water. She would acquit herself heroically. Bold as an Amazon, she stepped toward the gaze of the eager spectators, her heart swelling in her breast. She could not, would not let Claude down!

The clock ticked lugubriously. Nellie sat switching her tail, her yellow eyes fixed on the bathroom door. Agnes hovered behind her, wielding a plateful of Galaxy Cakes.

"Sophie, come on. You've got to come out of there sometime."

The bathroom door remained locked and impenetrable.

"I've got a treat for you. I found some Galaxies behind the ironing board."

"Don't mention food," wailed a muffled voice. "I'm ruined."

"Don't be silly. What did they expect when they just shoved you in front of that camera. You did the best you could."

Despairing moans pierced the door, making Nellie flatten her ears nervously. Agnes rattled the knob.

"It won't do any good imitating a wounded moose. Now open up. Nellie needs to get to her box."

After a long hesitation, the bolt creaked back and a woebegone face appeared in the opening. Sophie huddled in her bathrobe, eyes ringed with smudged mascara, a soldier broken on the field the first day of combat. Agnes snaked her hand in and nabbed her friend by the elbow.

"That's a good girl. Just a few more steps to the couch. Look at all this glorious chocolate goop waiting to be devoured!"

"I'm never going to eat again."

"You said the same thing after your Russian Policy exam and within the day you'd put away two giant pizzas and a yard-long submarine. You also passed the exam with flying colors!"

"Oh Agnes, that was just school. This is my career! My big chance. My first time in front of the CAM camera and what do I do, I make the worst, most absolute mess, the biggest fool of myself, the . . ."

"Enough!" Agnes shoved Sophie down on the couch in front of the cakes which she had thoughtfully sliced into bite-sized bits. "And don't go into your world-is-lost routine, because Nellie and I can't stand it. Now's the time for comfort food. Remember how Mary Lou Wallen used to stir half a bottle of ketchup into her milk whenever she got depressed?"

"I'm in worse shape than that!" Sophie stared morosely at the plate. "Agnes, when word of this gets out, I'll never be allowed a chance again. Never! I'm finished for good!"

Sophie remembered so clearly the shivery, fearful, glorious thrill that had shot through her as she walked out onto the set, heralded by Claude's theme music. Like a warrior, she had girded instantly for battle, ready to cope with any situation.

If only the situation hadn't involved cooking!

Gamely, the audience had greeted Sophie with applause as she gripped her emotions tightly after the turmoil of seeing Claude hurt. Laugh of laughs, she'd even bought into the idea that she could, in some small part, make up for the accident by filling the breach brave and true while Claude was out of action.

She had managed well—for about the first minute and a half. The time it took to introduce herself and announce that Mr. Lacomte had been, ". . . ah, unavoidably prevented from appearing."

Mournfully, Sophie eyed the Galaxy Cake and reached toward a sliver foaming with white filling. Comfort was comfort and she might as well take it wherever she could get it.

"It was just like walking into Frankenstein's lab, Agnes. All this stuff laid out and me with not the slightest idea what any of it was for or even what Claude was supposed to be making that day. Except that Martin said it was 'fish something.' ''

Sophie grimaced, remembering the shining pots, stainless steel bowls, razor-sharp chopping knives laid out before her.

"And then there was this cleaver," she went on. "Honest, you could have beheaded Mary Queen of Scots with it. And you know how I am with knives!"

Now Agnes did shudder. Knives were serious. By common consent, Sophie was not allowed near anything fiercer than a vegetable scraper.

Still caught in the heady intoxication of the lights, the cameras, and the concentrated attention of the audience, Sophie had only felt the first awful spurt of panic when she turned to the neatly arranged ingredients.

"Today we are making a . . . ah," Sophie again looked over the chopped veggies, the waiting stock, the whole sea bass that lay before her, glaring disapproval from its round, fishy eye.

Surely, she thought with a lurch, Claude hadn't intended to *clean* it in front of a live audience. Or maybe it was meant to be cooked as it was—though surely not. It was far too big to go whole into any of the pots.

"Look," Agnes patted Sophie's knee, "it couldn't have been any worse than those practice runs in journalism school. What matters is that you kept the people entertained and sent them away happy. Gord on security says he's never seen a jollier audience going out the door. Some were still laughing so hard . . ."

"Ohhhhh . . ."

"The tape'll be buried, erased. I think you deserve a medal for walking in cold and lasting out the time. I think Claude Lacomte ought to be darn grateful!" Agnes finished forcefully. "What does a little fish on the walls matter beside that?"

Sophie shrank into her bathrobe. On top of everything, she was really worried about Claude. She had tried phoning the hospital which said he was resting comfortably—and was adamant about no visitors. Why was he still at the hospital? Surely with a fracture, they just slapped a cast on and sent you home!

"How did I know it was so hard to get the head off a fish? How did I know the head was even supposed to come off? And it was so dratted . . . slippery!"

Taking the great cleaver in hand, Sophie had shut her eyes and chopped the creature into ragged vertical chunks. Those chunks that didn't fly violently off the counter she scraped onto a spatula and dumped into a great pot of pale broth that had been slowly simmering on one of the burners. Thus committed, she had picked up the rest of the ingredients and dropped them into the pot too, praying the plan had been for some kind of scaly stew.

She had, in fact, gotten all the way to the first commercial break before she realized that she had been acting in a sort of a daze, completely oblivious to the signals of the floor director, and to which of the three cameras was on. She was supposed to pause, then start up anew with the second segment of the show.

What second segment?

Sophie knew every moment of television time was carefully planned. No doubt Claude had done exactly that. In any other show, there would have been a script to read off the TelePrompTer, but all that had come up was a sort of shorthand Claude used to pace himself. The show was laid out in precisely timed visual blocks—all organized inside Claude's head.

Max was signaling frantically for Sophie to talk, act, tap-dance, do something to fill up the rest of the show. Sophie had to fill eleven minutes. Eleven minutes in which there appeared to be nothing more to do except stand in helplessly while the pot bubbled and frothed before her, a fishy devil's brew.

Since there were no more ingredients to be seen, Sophie cast desperately about in her mind for some cooking facts. Unable to find any, she started talking about the first thing that came into her mind—a frenzied monologue on the im-

portance of anchovies to the Peruvian economy, not omitting the ruin resulting in years when the anchovies
unaccountably disappeared.

The show had culminated with the stew boiling over
while Sophie made ineffectual matador passes with the pot
lid. At the wrap signal, she staggered from the dais, imbued
with a whole new respect for Claude, who endured the
ferocious pace, the blaze of attention time after time without turning into the blitzed wreck she was at that moment.

"Martin," she groaned. "Don't ever, ever do that to me
again."

Martin, who was helping the crew subdue the catastrophe
on the stove, swore vehemently that that was something
she never had to worry about for the next three lifetimes.

Agnes did manage, finally, to fill Sophie with Galaxy
Cakes, send her to bed, and even coax her in to work the
next morning. For the next two days, Sophie took a terrible
ribbing in the newsroom. However, as it was good-natured
ribbing, Sophie began to take heart. No one blamed her,
no one faulted her newsroom ability no matter what cracks
they made about her cooking disaster. This was exactly
what Sophie needed for her naturally resilient, scrappy
spirit to revive, a baptism of fire that admitted her to full
newsroom camaraderie. Everyone reminisced about their
own first experience. Even Greer, whom Sophie thought
just about perfect, confided that she had done her first live
newscast with a big piece of spinach stuck to her front
tooth.

"Don't worry so much," Greer had soothed. "All Martin needed was the audience entertained. You're lucky the
tape can be buried. If it ever got on the air—now that
would sink you."

Just to make sure, Sophie called programming twice.
Paula assured her that the slot would be filled with a repeat
of one of Claude's shows. Claude, by the way, had left the
hospital and remained cloistered in his apartment, still taking no calls. Word around the station was that he'd be
completely out of action for an unspecified time. His se-

clusion puzzled and worried Sophie. If he had only fractured his arm, why lock himself up like that? Was he hurt much worse than reports allowed? Or was Marianne nursing him so well he felt no inclination to do the show?

Sophie berated herself for the thought, but that didn't make it go away. She hadn't seen Marianne since way before Claude's mishap. As far as the studio knew, Marianne was still laid up with the flu. Marianne had better recover fast, for if Claude stayed incommunicado, it would be his assistant who would have to step into the taping breach.

Besides, if there was anyone Claude should demand care from, Sophie thought irrationally, it ought to be herself.

Grimly, Sophie put the whole thing out of her mind. Or tried to. When the time for the show rolled around, she flipped on the set to see what was going to be aired instead. To her horror, she saw the opening of the show and then herself walking on so blindly, so foolishly confident, the fish sprawled in front of her, her own hand reaching disastrously for the cleaver.

"Agnes," she shrieked. "Oh Agnes, tell me it isn't so!"

Agnes, who had been giving herself a henna treatment, dashed in, her hair in stiff green peaks under the ratty towel she kept for the purpose.

"Great Jehoshaphat!"

Even Agnes was rendered mute by the sight. And all the worse because, as the show careened drunkenly from disaster to disaster, she began to rock on the sofa, part of the towel stuffed against her mouth. Sophie was so rigid with shock at the sight on the screen, that it took her till the first commercial to spot what Agnes was doing.

"You're . . . laughing!" Sophie yelped. "I can't believe it. You, my best friend in the whole world. How can you?"

Agnes did make a heroic effort to stop. She bit her lips, held her breath, turned fuchsia, choked, sputtered, waved her hands in frantic apology, and finally, ended up, face down on the couch, her face stuffed into her prized CN Tower souvenir pillow to muffle the mirth coming out of her quivering body. Streaks of henna, unheeded, stained the fluffy pink sky printed around the needle-shaped Tower. Sophie snatched up the phone to find out what had happened. Paula was profusely apologetic.

"Look Sophie, it was another screwup. We had the repeat all lined up, but at the last minute, Roger spilled his coffee into it. So we grabbed the old episode of 'Tyke, Wonder Dog of the Yukon' we keep in case of dire emergency, but Martin comes screaming through that we hadn't paid up the syndication fees. Claude's other tapes were filed in Studio E and nobody had time to get one. It was either your tape or go to black!"

"I'm done for." Sophie actually started to tear her hair. "I bet the whole station is breaking up over it right now!"

"Practically rolling on the floor," Paula chortled mercilessly. "Hey, come on Sophie, you got to admit, it was really precious, you trying to chop up that fish. The phones started ringing before you were off the air."

Sophie completely missed the significance of this last remark until she arrived at work the following day. She was barely speaking to Agnes in spite of all Agnes's efforts to make up. She hadn't even time to get to her desk before she was hauled out of the barrage of newsroom humor and straight into Martin Scorley's cubbyhole, where a stack of pink message slips overflowed his boxing glove bookends.

"Whatever you did, you're some kind of a hit, Sophie. You're to do next week's show too."

"Oh no," Sophie yelped. "I couldn't do that. I couldn't. I'm with the newsroom, and Claude will be back by then."

"Doc says he'll be out of action for at least a month. If next week's as big a hit as this week, I say you get to do the whole month."

"What about Marianne? She could do it easily."

"The Buckeroo wants you."

"Mr. Owen!"

"Of course. You don't think I've got authorization to do something like this on my own?"

"Can't you run some repeats of what Claude has done? Or get Marianne to fill in at a pinch?"

"No repeats, no Marianne. Like I said, the boss wants you!"

There was no way Sophie could escape. When the Buckeroo spoke, you jumped or you left the station. And when Marianne finally rolled in, she was green and shaky and dropping into chairs as though her knees refused to support her.

"Claude said I had to get my bod in here and salvage something of the show or he'd shoot me personally. Right now, I can barely stand the thought of food. Claude is pretty upset about this, you know."

"I can guess," Sophie muttered. Only too well.

But at the back of her mind, one small cheery thought glimmered—at least Marianne hadn't been nursing Claude.

Chapter Seven

S ophie was sweating. How could a person sweat so much in front of a camera? If she didn't stop, her career as a future anchorwoman was doomed. Even as a reporter, she'd be good for nothing but dogsled races or blizzard patrol!

It's the studio lights, she told herself—and raw, naked fear! Sophie willed her pores to close. If she couldn't face a *boeuf tourtière*, how could she make it in the trenches of Beirut?

Drawing a deep breath, she picked up the rolling pin. It shouldn't be so hard, after all. She had rehearsed the sequence. The ingredients, chopped, marinated, pounded, or otherwise worked over, were laid out along the counter in order of use. If there was going to be a problem, it would be the pastry, but all the pastry had to do was hang together while she slapped it into the wide glass dish. Best of all, another *boeuf tourtière* was already baked and sitting at that very moment in the wall oven, plump and succulent, waiting only to be whipped out triumphantly at the end and displayed to the crowd. That Marianne, swaying woozily, had barely managed to construct it, was immaterial. It was only the eye that counted.

Methodically, Sophie began her struggle with the pastry which Marianne had already kneaded into a floury ball and left neatly reposing under a gingham cloth. As she worked, she tried not to think of Claude watching when the show was aired, glowering at her every move, catching her every slip.

104

When the dough tore straight across as she hoisted it over the *tourtière* dish, she covered with a desperate smile. Mustn't think about the word "slip!" You are what you think you are. Sophie went into her silent mantra: I am a wonderful cook, I am a wonderful cook, I am a wonderful cook.

She pushed the torn halves raggedly together in the bottom of the dish. Going into the second segment, she actually began to feel optimistic, save for an escaped onion rolling down the aisle, the show was progressing more or less okay. The pastry dough clung white and waiting. On the burner, the premixed filling bubbled satisfactorily. All Sophie had to do was dump it into the raw pastry shell, switch it with an identical one which Marianne had finished with a scalloped and ornamented pastry top, then, voilà, draw out the grand finale waiting in the oven.

Some of the filling in the pot must have spilled on the stove, Sophie thought, to account for the odd burning smell wafting up. The smell grew stronger, even after Sophie had dumped the filling into the *tourtière* shell. As she prepared to display Marianne's ready-to-cook model, she began to notice an uncomfortable stirring in the audience and wondered vaguely why, here and there, arms were beginning to wave. As she managed a neat switch with Marianne's handiwork, her heart lifted and she forgot the audience. At last! She was going to have a success!

Truly grateful, she wished she could share a smile with Marianne, but Marianne was stretched on the lunchroom couch, still chalky with flu.

"The oven!" a voice shouted. "The oven!"

Sophie's head snapped up. Max was making frenzied hand signals, though none Sophie recognized. He was pointing behind her. The wall oven was emitting a frill of smoke. The interior, through the glass window, was completely obscured with gray.

Oh no! Ignoring the myriad squawks of warning, Sophie yanked the oven door wide. Instantly, the set was flooded with acrid clouds while the *tourtière* Sophie pulled out, luckily remembering her oven mitts, resembled a relic from a nuclear test zone. Only then did Sophie realize what had happened. The *tourtière* had been precooked. There had been absolutely no need for her to turn the oven on at the start of the show!

The camera remained fixed relentlessly on Sophie's horrified expression while everyone waited to see what she would say. What Sophie said was forceful, spontaneous, and generally unfit for any public media. Well at least, Sophie thought, in the midst of the humiliating conflagration, they can't air this one. It's just too awful. I'm off the hook for good.

Air it they did—within two days. Sophie's caustic words were bleeped out but her expression only made the bleeps more effective than any actual words. Within five minutes of the show's finish, the switchboard was flooded—not with outrage, but with hordes of folk chortling, "Good for you Sophie! I've been saying exactly the same thing for years!"

Interest in "Ambrosia" jumped as though injected with steroids. Sophie was assigned "until further notice," newsroom duties suspended. Appalled, Sophie stormed the Buckeroo's office, an act of unheard-of daring. "I can't cook!" she pleaded, "I can scarcely boil water. I'm the last person you want in front of the camera out there!"

Before Claude's accident, Sophie could never have imagined herself making such a plea. Always, she had supposed she would do anything, *anything*, to get on air, including dancing a mamba on her hands. But she could not afford one more disastrous incident like that of the *tourtière*. She was messing up so badly her future was being blighted in the bud. She could not, would not jettison her dreams this way.

Behind a littered expanse of desk, the Buckeroo lounged, squat and dewlapped, his hair standing out in aggressive salt-and-pepper bristles. He looked like an aging commando who might jump up and butt his head through a brick wall at any moment. Nevertheless, he was grinning.

"You haven't a hope of getting out of it," he rasped cheerfully. "Not unless you want to be blackballed for the next twenty years. Face it, kiddo. You're a hit!"

"I'm not a hit! I'm a disaster. All those people just want to see me crash. Its mortifying!"

"Megacorp phoned. They want to buy two commercial spots on your show."

"I don't care who . . ."

Sophie screeched to a halt as the name of the huge conglomerate registered. Their ad revenues were pure gold and they rarely noticed the existence of small independents like CAM.

"If they come in, I can probably snag Benzer Pharmaceuticals and maybe even Flugel Foods." Jock actually rubbed his hands. "I've upped the rates already. You got all the makings of a money tree, kid. Me let you quit! Ha!"

His palm thumped the desk, making Sophie and several pencils jump. In spite of herself, Sophie was quelled into silence in the face of this ultimate measure of television success—the ability to attract paying sponsors. She didn't come back to her senses until Jock was hustling her out the door.

"But . . . I'm a reporter!" She tried vainly to dig in her heels. "I want to do something . . . real!"

"As of now, you got a raise. How's that for real?"

The door slammed behind Sophie. She didn't have a chance to rant until she was home with Agnes, where she paced furiously.

"I can't understand it. There are professional jokesters all over the place. People paid to be funny. Why doesn't the Buckeroo make a hit out of them? And," she added vehemently, "that nail polish you're using would stop a train!"

"Wouldn't it, though." Agnes surveyed her screaming toenails with pleasure and recapped the bottle. "I don't think you need to get worked up over the show. Don't you understand? It's not that you're making an idiot of yourself—though you are doing that too. It's that you're . . .

well, genuine! A flesh and blood woman who really can't cook. You appeal to the secret bumbler in all of us. No one deliberately encourages disaster on TV, but your disasters are hilarious. Not to mention that speech you made on bank rates while you were slicing the tomatoes. Even suave and sophisticated Claude couldn't have matched that!''

Claude had set up a tight schedule, and the Buckeroo meant Sophie to keep up the pace. Marianne, to her ever-lasting credit, dragged herself from her sickbed to help Sophie with the already planned productions. All thought of Marianne's possible relations to Claude vanished in the face of Sophie's profound gratitude to see help, any help, on the horizon. Her greatest concern was that Marianne's virus seemed settled in for the duration, turning her ashen several times a day.

"I don't think you should be out of bed," Sophie had ventured. "You look . . ."

"Like fettuccine warmed over. I know. I feel that way too, but I want to do what I can for Claude's show."

Sophie smothered a prick of feeling at this loyalty to Claude. Marianne did her best. She simplified the dishes, tried to explain Claude's complicated equipment and even, heaven help her, Claude's food philosophy. Sophie discovered an unsuspected and horrifying new world of glazes, pasta al dente, markets open before dawn, and fourteen-piece place settings. She did two more shows, and even with Marianne doing her best, the results came out the same. The first time, she dropped the herring salad she had just spent twenty minutes making. The second time, despite Marianne's gestures, Sophie turned on the blender without the lid, spewing raspberry sauce over the studio ceiling. Yet Martin wouldn't let Marianne near the camera despite Sophie's pleas.

"When is Claude going to get back," Sophie groaned. "When?"

Sophie alternately quaked in anticipation of his return and longed for it as relief for her own plight. She knew he was outraged at her fumblings, for his howls could almost be heard in the halls. He'd been in communication with everyone with a shred of influence in his efforts to alter the situation. Everyone but Sophie, to whom he seemed determined never to speak again.

Yet Claude remained walled up in his apartment, having security block would-be visitors, especially after a horde of eager busybodies had tried to get his reaction to Sophie's show, A fractured arm was a fractured arm—but Claude acted as though he were concealing evidence of the bubonic plague.

He was especially incommunicado to Sophie, who was simultaneously in a rage about being forced to do the cooking show, and in a torment of conscience about the injuries she had inflicted upon the man. Worst of all, she was in a torment of curiosity about what was going on in his apartment and why her best efforts had failed to pry loose his unlisted phone number. Her imagination treated her to a vision of the man writhing on a bed of pain while she wrecked everything he had been working for. She had to go see him for herself. Even though she might get eaten, at least she would have bearded the lion in his den.

Flowers got Sophie into Claude's building. Flowers, ingenuity and a borrowed delivery jacket let Sophie bluff her way past security, up the elevator to Claude's door. Before her nerve could weaken, she rapped smartly, making sure the flowers obscured the peephole. From inside, she heard a mutter, a curse, then something slow and heavy scraping toward her—a sound straight out of *Curse of the Mummy's Tomb*. At least . . . he can walk, she told herself over the prickling of her scalp.

"Who is it?" Claude called curtly, ready to fling any possible visitors off the balcony.

"Floral delivery, sir."

The thumping drew closer. Mutters penetrated the wood as Claude unlocked the door and opened it a crack. Making bold use of her floral shield, Sophie thrust herself inside.

"You!" Claude flared. "What are you doing here?"

"What's it look like! Bringing comfort to the wounded."

Through the flowers, Sophie at first saw only Claude's glowering face. Then her gaze traveled to the rest of him. Claude's right wrist was in a cast and sling. This made things difficult for his left hand, which was gripping a crutch. The crutch precariously supported Claude on his good left leg. His right leg hung, encased, hip to ankle, in a contraption of straps and braces surely invented by the Inquisition. He stood grimly while Sophie took in the whole picture and grew pale at the apparent extent of Claude's injuries.

"What is that!" She pointed, aghast, certain he had been maimed for life.

Grudgingly, Claude explained that there was nothing wrong with his leg save a damaged nerve sheath that needed a few weeks to repair itself. Until then, the least wrong move was excruciating—hence the medieval device keeping the leg immobile.

Forcible confinement hadn't done much for Claude himself, Sophie noticed. His cheekbones stood out tautly and his eyes fairly snapped with restlessness and frustration. The mere sight of Sophie made him bristle all over like a prodded porcupine.

"I suppose you've been sent with another apology! For putting me out of action and wrecking my show!"

Sophie had been prepared for considerable crankiness on Claude's part. Goodness knows, he had reason. Now his very nearness stirred the hairs on the back of her neck. She'd better counter him while she still had some contrition left.

"You had your part in knocking over the backdrop too," she pointed out, "stepping toward me like that. And as for wrecking your show, what else did you expect when I got shoved on the set with about thirty seconds notice!"

Without deigning to answer, Claude plunked the door shut. Sophie wondered whether she imagined it or she really felt the heat of his breath on her cheek. She turned,

looking around for a place to set down the flowers. Halfway
to a narrow glass table, she uttered a soft, sharp, "Oh!"

What had arrested her was the interior of Claude's apartment, which certainly shared no resemblance to the modest
digs she and Agnes inhabited. She was hard put not to
simply gape around, avid in spite of herself, for what the
home revealed of the man.

A man spare, simple, at ease with himself, yet who lived
amidst luxury spread with the easy touch of someone who
knows its facets intimately. Color and texture showed a
Claude with senses fully alive. The warmth of the bamboo-
papered walls, the handwoven Iranian rugs, the great deep
tobacco upholstered sofas and chairs, somehow made
Sophie feel as though Claude's hands had reached out and
caressed her. A collection of hockey masks over the fire-
place added something tribal, while on the coffee table lay
a huge, half-assembled jigsaw puzzle which Sophie knew
instantly Claude hadn't wanted her to catch him at.

Only after several moments did Sophie realize how she
had been staring at everything. Or rather absorbing every
detail in that way she had when her attention was truly
aroused.

"I'm glad I'm not in a car with you," Claude drawled.
"You'd probably be running us over an embankment right
now instead of merely wreaking havoc on the set."

Some of his initial grouchiness seemed to have retreated
as he watched Sophie's fascination with his living space.
Belatedly, Sophie snapped out of her trance, wondering
why she was unable to stop being so confoundedly curious
about the man.

"I did my best on short notice!"

"That was obvious. But you kept coming back again—
with the results worse and worse."

"It wasn't my idea. The Buckeroo insisted!"

"I know," Claude replied darkly. "I was on the phone
the moment I heard about it. 'Not going to squelch a good
thing when it falls into my lap' was how Owen put it. He
seems to enjoy using a comedienne!"

Sophie felt herself beginning to breathe rapidly. The flowers dropped from her fingers to the table. She might not be able to cook, but she regarded herself as an intelligent professional and she had given "Ambrosia" her best. She meant never, no matter what she did, to be regarded as a clown. The hint, the breath of such a thing, spelled certain death in her chosen field and stirred up all the indignation she possessed.

"I am not a clown!" she fired back. "I gave that show my best shot and I'll continue to do so as long as they force me . . ."

Her words trailed off at Claude's expression.

"What do you mean, as long as they force you?"

"Megacorp is buying commercial spots. To attract that kind of money, the Buckeroo will run a dancing donkey on the show!"

"A dancing donkey!" The expression on Claude's face could have made Sophie either laugh or cry. "Then why did he bother hiring me?"

With an opening like that, how could Sophie resist? Her anger evaporated and she gave Claude a glance that took in the whole delectable maleness of him, from his unruly hair to the strong bare calves under his dressing gown. Oh yes! cried something deep within her, as every cell suddenly hummed with response to the physical man. Agnes had been perfectly right.

"Because he's not a fool, Claude. He knows a hunk when he sees one. Sure you're a celebrity. Sure you've got credentials. But all those would mean nothing unless you also had, as dear Agnes puts it, twenty-four-karat sex appeal. That's what hauls in the audiences. You could have been making mud pies and no one would care as long as it paid off for the station. It's not," she couldn't prevent herself from adding, "as though it were something that depended on plain hard facts—like the news."

These truths were self-evident to Sophie—but not, apparently, to Claude. He began to turn such a vivid shade that Sophie grew alarmed. Even the healthiest of men, in their prime, could be felled by a heart attack.

"Thank you," he finally ground out, "for the lesson in media reality. It'll save me wasting any more breath on the Buckeroo."

"Well, you needed it, standing on camera in your stark white outfit making concoctions no earthly mortal could put together. Why else do you think so many people were watching you?"

For a moment, Claude stared out the window with the look of a man stranded on a desert island and wondering when rescue is going to appear. Then his gaze swung back to Sophie. A betraying muscle twitched at the side of his mouth—in an instant, cracking the rigidity of the rest of his face. A humorous snort forced its way out, nearly causing him to lose his grip on the crutch.

"You do it for me every time, Sophie Moore. Just when I'm so infuriated with you, you come out with something like that. I mean . . . oh . . ." he hitched sharply to keep from toppling sideways, "who else would walk up to a man and tell him deadpan that he's nothing but a sex object!"

"I never said you were *just* a sex object!"

Though, heaven knew, that part of him was certainly true.

"Oh, I see. I suppose I ought to be thankful for that!"

Claude snorted again, caught his breath, and looked Sophie up and down keenly. "Tell me," he inquired in a different, more dangerous tone, "Do you plan to make it on sex appeal too, since skill as a chef seems to count for naught?"

"That!" Sophie spat, "doesn't even deserve an answer!"

It wasn't his question, but the sudden flare in his eyes that sparked such an instant retort. What Sophie meant was that she couldn't possibly make it on sex appeal, that she was too ordinary, that she never gave the matter a thought—except when Claude stood agitating her hormones like that. Oh, how did this conversation get so wildly out of her control!

The muscle at the corner of Claude's mouth grew firm again. He took a step closer to Sophie, who found herself strangely unable to move, even when the contraption on Claude's leg scraped across the hardwood like a body dragged in the night.

"Perhaps," he continued, with velvety meaning, "I underestimated the strength of your ambition. Maybe you did knock that set over on me just to get your chance in front of a camera. You told me about it yourself over that abominable lunch."

Two echoing thuds brought Claude closer yet, so close Sophie could see that the figures on his burgundy silk dressing gown were tiny griffins and his chest seemed to be bare underneath it. Some tendon weakened in her knees at the thought.

"Why is it," she rapped out in self-defense, "that you just can't prevent yourself from baiting me when you have the chance?"

A half-explosive sound heaved at his chest and he spoke through teeth set in what might have been a grimace or a grin.

"Maybe I can't help myself. You're like a burr in my tail. I have to keep at it and at it until I get it out!"

Slow lava began to bubble in Sophie's veins. She had come to offer aid, succor, and reasonable explanations, but Claude was rapidly putting an end to all that. Swiftly, she stepped away from him, her shoulder brushing a wall sculpture which rattled precariously in its expansive brackets.

"I really came to finish what I was saying on the set. That tape I made at Mallory's, the one you got so steamed about, Greer took it to the police. And the film too. She won't tell me any details, but I think, I just think I got something that might help get the McCloskys off the hook."

Now that she was back to a topic she understood, Sophie's demeanor changed, infused once again with the excitement of the chase. Claude hesitated, but was unable to resist the question.

"Didn't you listen to the tape first?"

"No. I . . . ah, it slipped my mind till I actually got to work."

Claude's eyes narrowed and, suddenly, the kiss at the door loomed up between them. Though neither said a word, the reason that Sophie hadn't listened to the tape seemed glaringly obvious.

"How good," Claude asked, "was that recorder anyway?"

"Best I could buy. I have to have decent tools, you know."

"Then . . . our conversation was likely on it too!"

So that was why Greer had looked at her so queerly. Sophie turned brilliant scarlet.

"I . . . hadn't thought of that," she said faintly. "You didn't . . . I mean . . . what did you say, anyway?"

Now why, *why*, did she have to come out with that! Sophie's pulse began to pound in her ears like a kettle drum even as the flush working up Claude's neck told that it had been, most definitely, the wrong thing to say.

"Don't you remember?"

"I . . . was all caught up trying to keep track of Hooper."

After a moment of utter incredulity, Claude's features gathered into a scowl out of which his eyes blazed greenly. His short, barking laugh had very little humor attached.

"I guess the joke's on me, then. So much for making an impression!"

"But you did make an impression," Sophie blurted. "I . . ."

Her teeth snapped shut, almost biting her tongue. Since Claude's brows immediately began to climb, almost comically at odds with the scowl on the rest of his face, Sophie decided to hold her ground. Her jaw squared, her gaze never left Claude's face for all the intense heat plucking at the roots of her hair.

Charged silence hung between the pair, in which Sophie

could hear the thin wail of a siren and the creak of the wooden crutch as Claude shifted slightly. Now he seemed to be trying to read her, his gaze sliding heatedly over Sophie's skin.

"Was it this kind of impression?" he inquired at last.

And with amazing litheness for a fellow on one good leg, he was beside her, lowering his lips on hers, tasting her, caressing her, sending exquisite little starts of joy along her nerve ends. Sophie swayed toward him, caught up in the smoky sensuality the man could spread around her like an intoxicating cloud. Her lids fell shut and her head tilted back. In a last ditch effort to save herself from the honeyed whirlpool, she stepped sideways. Claude followed, rashly forgetting his invalid status. One second later, he went crashing in a heap to the floor.

"You did that one to yourself!" Sophie told him after she had hauled him upright again and fled to the door. Burr in his tail indeed!

Sophie continued to cling to the idea that her salvation would come when Claude was back on his feet and back on the set. Then he could be as blessedly high-toned as he liked. He could make orchid soup and unicorn pie for all Sophie cared so long as she, thank all the lucky stars in the sky, was back in the newsroom, getting on with her life at last.

Eventually, Claude did appear, favoring his right leg and missing a good deal of his tan. News of his arrival raced through CAM like gusts before a hurricane. By the time Sophie heard about it, Claude was in the Buckeroo's office. By the time Sophie was speeding down the hall, he was out of the Buckeroo's office again, the hall vibrating with the thud of the door.

"Congratulations!" Claude gritted when the two all but collided in front of the west water fountain.

Sophie was so startled that, for one unbalanced moment, she actually wondered whether he were approving her performances. This mad impression was further reinforced

when he reached out and took her hand, shaking it with
grave formality.

"Congratulations," he continued. "You have now got
complete control of 'Ambrosia.' "

"No I don't," Sophie replied ingenuously. "You're
back."

"Only long enough to turn in my resignation—which
your good leader has in his hands right now."

"Resign! But I thought . . . you liked this show. You certainly got emotional enough about it when I came to see
you."

Claude seemed to uncoil like a tall steel spring, a muscle
in his cheek jumping as he looked at Sophie.

"Oh, I get emotional about a lot of things, but that's not
why I'm quitting. Charming as you are, I have professional
standards to keep. I refuse to be cohost with a lady who
thinks that omelettes boil."

"Cohost?"

"That's what the Buckeroo demanded. I had to insist on
using the parachute clause in my contract."

"But . . . what'll you do?"

For the first time, Claude grinned that devil-inspired grin.

"Why, make use of everything I've learned from you,
of course. Fame and fortune ought to be no trick at all!"

His finger traced her cheek, feather light. Then he was
gone.

Chapter Eight

The kitchen was practically gone too. Sophie arrived to find the set naked to the countertops, the hooks bare, the deep shelves for pots and bowls gaping emptily at her.

"Oh, didn't they tell you?" Max exclaimed. "All the equipment was Claude's. He took it with him."

"Marianne! Where's Marianne?"

"Gone too. She was always part of Claude's package deal."

Inside of two minutes, a panic-stricken Sophie was in the Buckeroo's office.

"How soon are you going to get Claude replaced?"

Jock, catching the bottom of a ball game on his office set, hitched at his suspenders. He favored suspenders for their flavor of sawdusty bars and manly bulldog jowls gripping cigars.

"He's already replaced. Show's all yours, kiddo!"

Sophie lurched out of the office—and into a number of dreadful developments. First, she was permanently relieved from the newsroom. Next, a contract appeared, designating her host of "Ambrosia." Then her salary actually took a hop up the scale.

"What am I going to do," Sophie groaned to Agnes. "I can't, I just can't keep making an idiot out of myself on that show."

"Did you beg and plead as piteously as you could?"

"I groveled on the carpet. Didn't have the least effect!"

"Then don't sign. Tell the Buckeroo what to do with his contract. Quit!"

Heartlessly, Agnes grinned. They both knew what would happen should Sophie balk at the show. The Buckeroo would fire her. When other stations discovered she had walked out on opportunity, she'd be labeled unreliable, even a troublemaker. No one would take a chance on her the second time around. Refusal spelled ruin. So did acceptance. Once Sophie got established as the culinary klutz of Toronto, was there any way she could go back to her true career? Who would ever take her seriously again!

"You know I can't quit," Sophie fretted. "Even if I have to keep egg on my face for a whole year, there's no way I'm going to pull a kamikaze stunt like walking out!"

Seeing Sophie about to sink genuinely into the depths of despair, Agnes began to look wise.

"This really isn't like you, Soph. Most people would jump with glee over such a bit of luck. What you have to do is look upon it as a challenge, your big break! Why don't you just surprise them all and show what you can do?"

Agnes knew how to apply bracing medicine. After only twenty minutes of haranguing, Sophie's eyes began to gleam with visions of vindication and even glory—especially when Agnes mentioned Claude. She signed the contract and flung herself headlong into conquering the airwaves from behind a kitchen stove.

And Lola Mallow pounced on the change.

"Congratulations to Sophie Moore, the ambitious lady who knocked the set over on Claude Lacomte and ended up permanently stealing the show. She can't poach an egg without mishap—but no matter. She's got enterprise and that's what counts. Perhaps that's why Claude's elegant tail is in a knot . . ."

So! Lola must have been talking to Claude—who apparently hadn't stinted his opinions on the matter. Sophie would have thought sour grapes was hardly his style.

*   *   *

When the shock of Claude's departure finally made itself felt at CAM, a collective sigh went up from the female staff and those of the crew who had grown plump on Claude's show. Even in the general madhouse of the newsroom, Claude's presence was missed. And missed, maddeningly enough, most acutely by Sophie.

It's just that I want my old job, she grumbled, chin in hand, lamenting the action she was missing. Yet it wasn't only the newsroom that filled her mind, but Claude's face leaning close, the easy way he strolled in step with her, the lively spice of his conversation, even the way that flush climbed his face when he finally lost his temper. Something indefinably vital had gone away. Without Claude, the station seemed to have a hole in it, an emptiness that echoed even in the busiest halls.

Nothing was heard of Claude. He might as well have gone to Mars. Sophie tried to blot out the probability that he'd headed back to Montreal, to his hotel, out of her life for good. The idea wrenched at her. In spite of all their clashes, she'd really thought . . .

What had she really thought?

Sophie plucked at a fern without noticing she was pulling off bits. She'd really thought Claude was . . . well, attracted to her. That his teasing, his laughter, even his flashes of temper meant she held a special interest for him. Yet now he had simply waltzed off with nary a trace left behind.

"The nerve!" she spluttered to an empty lounge—then clamped her jaw, chagrined to find she had erupted aloud. This had gone further than even she had suspected. She had better put a stop to it at once! Just a case of chemicals bouncing off each other, she told herself forcefully. It could have gotten messy. I ought to be thankful for such an easy escape!

Ha! taunted the rude little voice at the back of her mind. Some narrow escape if all you've got to show for it is one night on the town and a couple of lousy kisses!

Claude hadn't disappeared. Within three weeks he was in the public eye again, preceded, of course, by Lola

Mallow looking smug enough to have swallowed a whole shopful of canaries.

"It's onward and upward for Claude Lacomte, recent escapee from CAM TV. The long-planned gourmet lifestyle feature at CXRT has fallen into the hands of our sexy chef. Hold onto your throbbing hearts, ladies, and be watching tomorrow at five!"

To Sophie, the shock was almost worth it just to see the fury of the Buckeroo, who had refused to hand "Ambrosia" back to Claude free and clear. Everyone at CAM was jammed around assorted monitors when "Chez Claude" came on. Sophie and Agnes had managed to get the cubbyhole of a coffee room to themselves where they huddled, transfixed by what they saw.

Claude Lacomte was no longer Claude the expert chef, but Claude, raconteur, bon vivant, and devastating man about town. Gone was the stiff white jacket, the kitchen of a thousand culinary devices, the Claude who spoke in serious complexities. That Claude had been replaced by a roguish fellow completely at ease with himself and smiling at the camera as though it were an instrument solely designed to bring Claude's fascinating activities to the world. The very first closeup, featuring Claude's raffish smile and backed by sensuous cello theme music, got the message across indeed!

The new format was clear, too—a format that could only have been of Claude's own invention in its daring simplicity. Claude was to have a guest, who was to be pampered, entertained, and otherwise cosseted throughout the hour by Claude. His set, in warmest sienna, gold, and burgundy, announced itself as a bachelor hideaway—personal, intimate, smacking of pleasurably wicked assignations. Food was incidental. The purpose of the show seemed simply to stun each viewer with Claude's potent masculine charisma.

The premiere of "Chez Claude" featured Jasmine Erle, popular star of a daytime TV soap, who floated around Claude like sultry smoke, laughing her famous laugh and flirting gaily. Claude reciprocated, teasing her back and asking the sort of questions that allowed Ms. Erle to reveal her career plans, her tastes in ice cream, her opinions on saving the wetlands of Ontario. Interspersed were clips of the two of them at the Farmer's Market shopping for bell peppers, mugging over hand-glazed teapots, and sharing a café au lait afterward in the cosiest of sidewalk cafés.

While the two acted like lovers out on a lark, Claude managed, by sheer sleight of hand, to whip up *crêpes Normandie* and offer them up to Ms. Erle with the air of a chieftan flinging treasure at the feet of a visiting queen. Jasmine Erle responded by tasting the crepes as though she were tasting Claude himself. From the glint in her eye, one knew she had no intention of giving up the chase after the camera was done.

Each time Claude had glanced toward the camera, he had seemed to be grinning at Sophie, saying, here's what I can do if I choose to put my mind to it! Just top this!

"He's good," Sophie ground out through her molars as the closing credits began, "very good indeed!" Her fist crushed a Styrofoam cup into powdery rubble. She emitted a muffled, grittily satisfying tumble of words.

"What?" Agnes turned, startled at Sophie's glowering fury.

"Look at you!" Sophie burst out. "Mesmerized by the guy! That show has nothing to do with cuisine—and everything to do with Mr. Claude's rippling manliness. That's not a food show! That's pure seduction on tape! And he's doing it to get my goat!"

The absurdity of this last statement made Sophie pause only fractionally. "Well he is!" she crashed on defiantly. "He was mad about leaving CAM. And you think this is a big step up!"

"I never said a word," Agnes protested.

"You were the one who told me on the first day that all a host needed was sex appeal!"

"But that was just . . ."

"And you're wondering just how soon he's going to

wipe me off the map. After all, if we're comparing
assets . . .''

"Sophie! You're raving!"

The rush of sympathy in Agnes's eyes brought Sophie
to a skidding halt. Grabbing up her purse, she stomped off
outside. When she really got in a lather, she had to walk it
off—and this one warranted at least twenty miles of blis-
tering speed.

So Claude had got a new station, a new format, a new
show. She ought to be glad for him. Why did it fling her
into a rage?

Or was she simply having a fit of jealousy!

Sophie cringed, for the word was not one in her vocab-
ulary. Yet hadn't Claude moved his career, his fledgling
career, way past hers in merely the space of a summer,
nonchalantly pulling off something Sophie expected to take
years accomplishing for herself in her chosen field.

She brushed this off as an unworthy thought, even
though she was the one with the journalism degree, the one
who had slugged her way through political science . . .

"Rats!" she shouted at a pigeon who dared land beside
her. It wasn't Claude's career she was so stirred up about.
It was the way he'd lavished his charm and himself on the
alluring Ms. Erle and the camera so impersonally. A charm
she had grown accustomed to thinking of, in a chaotic, half-
unconscious, but very powerful way, as somehow being
special for her. So much for that! The man had turned himself deliberately into a public property. The act of an ego
taller than the Matterhorn—just like Stan. Men! You
couldn't take a single one seriously!

The more Sophie mulled this over, the more ragged she
grew inside—with no plausible reason except that she too
had been caught by the honeyed lure.

"Ridiculous!" she exclaimed even as Claude's smile
swam into her memory. Fear touched her. She couldn't,
wouldn't fall into some silly infatuation with green eyes
and wicked double dimples. So what if he also admired
Nellie McClung and could hold his own discussing postwar

Afghanistan. So what if he had biteable earlobes and . . .
oh, no! Why did the fellow have to be distilled attraction
on wheels!

Occupied with squelching this bubbling brew of emotions, Sophie failed to reckon on the Buckeroo, at his most
belligerent, stomping the next day into Studio E.

"As of Monday," he growled, " 'Ambrosia' is going
daily. I'll get you another assistant, whatever you need. Just
whomp the pants off Claude Lacomte!"

Daily! The pace would kill her. Or perhaps her spectacular expiry on camera was the Buckeroo's idea of whomp-
ing Claude. When the Buckeroo left, Sophie snatched up a
saucepan and slammed it to the floor with all her might.
Claude's fault! Somehow everything had become Claude's
fault. She'd get back to the newsroom now.

Claude, naturally, chose this moment to phone and ask
her opinion of his CXRT debut. Sophie could barely believe he was asking such a thing in that easy, straightfor-
ward voice of his. Not after all the silence. Not after getting
her trapped into a daily show. Not after letting Jasmine Erle
swarm all over him while the whole province watched. She
began to hyperventilate.

"You should have asked my opinion before you decided
to turn yourself into the biggest goodie on the air!"

"Whew!" Claude whistled. "Aren't we a little prickly.
I must have been a big hit at CAM!"

"Is that why you called? To find out?"

"Not really," Claude replied after a moment. "Perhaps
I just wanted to hear your voice."

Sophie's mind threw up the myriad occasions on which
he could have heard her voice had he made the faintest
effort. Her heart, all by itself, started thudding so hard she
couldn't trust herself to speak. Claude picked up her rasp
of breath and sought for neutral ground.

"Ah . . . I also wanted to ask about the McCloskys. I feel
that you and I have a sort of personal interest in their fate."

A question that was fire touched to gunpowder.

"I don't know," Sophie blazed. "I'll probably never

know because now I'm chained to the counter in Studio E. Because of you, the Buckeroo is making 'Ambrosia' go daily!''

There was another pause in which Sophie's fevered imagination pictured Claude doing everything from choking back astonishment that anyone would give her the responsibility to smothering wild laughter at the very idea.

"I hope you're suitably amused," she burst out. "I hope you're flattered that . . .''

"Sophie!''

Sophie lapsed heavily into silence.

"Look, Sophie, I caught you at a bad time. I was just going to . . . never mind. I'll call back when you're in a better mood."

"You were going to what? *What?*'' Sophie cried into the receiver, but Claude had hung up. Sophie hung up too, helplessly racked with disappointment at whatever it was she had missed.

She acquired two food assistants; not the battle-hardened veterans she so desperately needed, but Beth and Joel, callow, overawed youngsters the Buckeroo had snatched newly hatched and cheap from the hospitality course of the nearby community college. At the sight of them, Sophie might have crumbled completely save for rousing speeches from Agnes and hourly injections of Galaxy Cakes.

When she realized she was waiting, actually *waiting* for a return call from Claude, Sophie finally got into gear. "I'll show him!" she declared. "I will!"

"Showing Claude" was going to take some doing. His show was an instant hit, its audience share zooming skyward from the very first week, proving all over again that a lopsided grin and a laugh like warm honey were supremely marketable. All Sophie's competitiveness came out. She resembled a snub-nosed tugboat butting its way obsessively through a North Atlantic gale. Even Martin Scorley, who had made an attempt to rise to the occasion, bounced off Sophie's all-out assault on the show. Soon he realized that Sophie, like Claude, was another cushy assignment and he'd best stay out of the way in the local bar.

Despite increased staff, the sweat of the assistants, and Sophie's best efforts, disaster after disaster continued to plague the show. Sauces burned, cakes collapsed, and appliances revolted until she could only conclude that the universe was out to make a permanent joke of her. Yet, no matter what she did, calls and letters continued to flood in. Her audience share climbed steadily too. The Buckeroo started to grin again. He grinned especially wide whenever Sophie tried to escape.

"Look at the ad revenue, kiddo. You're manna from heaven. Just between you and me, without 'Ambrosia,' the bank would have had us belly-up end of the next quarter. You wouldn't want to see all your friends out of a job!"

So that's why the wily old badger had wanted to go daily, Sophie thought. He could sell the ad spots high and rake in a bundle! As for the bankruptcy threat, who really knew? It was nice to be thought of as a savior. On the other hand, she didn't trust one inch that devious glint in the Buckeroo's eye.

"But look what's in the ads," Sophie complained, lamenting the treachery of the large companies greeted so joyfully but weeks before, "They're all for laxatives and stomach upset remedies. 'Chez Claude' never lets us forget it!"

War had broken out between the two shows. Sophie couldn't have said how—save that the pair seemed destined for mortal combat from very beginning. Lola Mallow stirred the pot continuously, oozing all over Claude, slyly harping on the idea that Sophie secretly drooled over her rival as much as the rest of the female population.

"Now that Claude Lacomte," Lola purred, "has learned to cash in on the dynamite sex appeal nature provided, will dear clumsy Sophie be able to stand it? It's known for a fact she now regrets having run such a luscious hunk out of her territory and into the paths of women who seem much more appreciative . . ."

Sophie had been prevented, only by a flying tackle by Agnes, from ringing Lola personally and scorching the woman's ear off.

"Do you want to total yourself completely?" Agnes had squawked, wresting the receiver away. "Do you want to be displayed in tiny hacked-up pieces all over Lola's show?"

Stone-jawed, Sophie had relinquished the phone. Not only was there a rule at CAM that no one ever, on pain of thumbscrews and the rack, speak to Lola Mallow, but she knew that one hint of how irate she really was would keep Lola gloating for weeks.

Meanwhile, Claude's show continued to both fascinate her and drive her round the bend. Claude seemed to be doing nothing on the air but having fun—something that offended Sophie's sense of the gravity of broadcasting. Added to this was his ongoing, effortless way with female guests. A . . . frivolous man altogether!

CXRT didn't care what Claude did on air. They only knew they had a good thing on their hands. Very soon, the station trusted Claude to do his show live, so that the last twenty minutes could be a phone-in portion, allowing viewers to question Claude and his guests directly.

The viewers weren't interested in the food. They were interested in the guests, they were interested in Claude— and above all they were interested in Claude and Sophie.

There was plenty to ask about. After a bit of initial restraint, salvos had begun flying about like cannonballs at the Battle of Waterloo. Sophie couldn't say who had begun—though she suspected it was herself, after the buildup of speculation and innuendo broke her control and made her rashly comment on puffed-up male TV personalities. Lola snatched it up with glee.

"Our sweet Sophie is feeling the sting. And who wouldn't, watching the string of lovelies cooing over toothsome Claude. For relief, Sophie can always resort to the products of her sponsors—good for heartburn whatever the cause!"

"Ignore her!" Agnes begged, guarding the telephone with her body. "It's the oldest trick in the book, whipping up a romantic interest between public personalities. How else do you think the scandal sheets have survived all these years?"

"First you have to have the darn romance!" Sophie shouted. "And Lola hasn't got one scrap of evidence!"

"She thinks she's got all the evidence she needs—just from looking at your faces!"

Despite Sophie's attempts at rigid control, the series of potshots escalated—Sophie's direct and just this side of libel, Claude's answers in the form of such oblique and smooth asides that Sophie could never find the wound on herself even though she was sure she had just been neatly pinged.

She would take no calls from Claude—not that he tried very hard after the CAM switchboard cut him off. He resorted to other methods of expression—such as the courier who arrived at Sophie's apartment all but smothered by an enormous armful of roses. Under the roses had been a steaming, perfect shrimp teriyaki, the very dish Sophie had botched on air that day.

"This is just too much!" Sophie cried in the astonished courier's face. The teriyaki was just another way to twit her about her unhappy kitchen skills. And the flowers, which had given Sophie such an involuntary leap of pleasure, now looked just like the bouquet Sophie had used to bluff her way into Claude's apartment. Agnes fought off Sophie's attempt to hurl the teriyaki across the room, protesting, quite in vain, that maybe Claude was trying to give her a present. They compromised by catching the courier and making him take the teriyaki and the roses straight back where they came from.

Claude continued to enjoy himself on air—irritating Sophie the most by the way he dealt with the rising number of phone-in callers who begged him to have Sophie as a guest.

"A face-to-face with that lady is a test for strong men

and delicate digestions," Claude would purr, voice dripping with so many kinds of meaning even the most obtuse viewer could pick them up. "Ms. Moore is welcome here any time."

He fended off other questions with infuriating aplomb and a highwayman's grin. And, as though to make good his words, he showed up outside CAM one squally evening, waylaying Sophie as she began her dash homeward in the rain. He leaned over and pushed open the passenger door of the Porsche.

"Been waiting for you," he said against the wind. "Get in."

The last gleams of day caught the slash of his profile, making Sophie's surprised pulse set up a clamor. The warm interior of the car beckoned. A lean masculine hand reached to help her in. Sophie backed away.

"Why? Didn't you get enough digs in at me today?"

"I came to ask you to guest on my show."

Claude mistook Sophie's speechlessness for hesitation and pushed the door open further.

"Get in out of the rain and let's talk about it."

"Are you kidding! In this neighborhood somebody'll see us together and I'll never live it down. I suppose you've already been working on the Buckeroo!"

Pulling her umbrella down over her head, Sophie stepped around the tail of the car and started across the street. She heard the passenger door chunk shut and the motor start. Before she knew it, the Porsche was at her side and Claude leaning out the driver's window.

"I haven't been working on anyone, Sophie. I came specifically to ask in person. And to give you," he added somewhat bitingly, "the chance to answer in person without stirring up a whole hive at CAM."

Sophie only continued to walk faster, but her top speed was no match for the Porsche.

"Look, come over and see what it's like. You can come now, after hours, just for a look around."

"I can't even believe you're asking these things."

Sophie stumbled on a storm grate. "What's the matter! Haven't had your strong-man test this week?"

The Porsche snarled closer, barely avoiding a puddle that would have drenched its quarry. Claude was now gripping the wheel with all his knuckles.

"You've been a test since the moment I met you!" he shouted over the swash of the windshield wipers. "Now stop being an idiot about all this. I don't know what you think I've been doing but . . ."

"Forget it, Claude! The answer is no!"

Sophie peeled sharply into an indoor shopping arcade, with only time to see the Porsche hesitate, then accelerate away. "Wait!" she cried suddenly, but it was too late. Standing among the shoppers, Sophie felt forlorn. The hollowness persisted in her bosom right up until the next edition of "Show Bits" in which Lola announced that Claude had been seen in the vicinity of CAM probably extending an invitation to his rival.

"What will come of this assignation between our famous pair?" Lola wanted to know. "Will we soon see Sophie dropping pots on Claude's toes? Will she prove any more impervious to the lure of Claude's hideaway than his other feminine guests?"

So much for considerate private inquiry! Claude would resort to any currency to keep the spotlight on himself! The Buckeroo laughed heartily at Sophie's indignation.

"Give him as good as you get, kid!" was his advice. "Why else have you got your own show?"

This attitude, highly unprofessional as it seemed, appealed strongly to the combative side of Sophie's nature. And the Buckeroo, she knew, loved nothing more than a good scrap. Flinging away her last shreds of restraint, Sophie submerged her other feelings for Claude in the adrenaline rush of battle.

Or what would have been a rush had she ever seemed to win. Arguing with Claude in the rain brought on a dreadful head cold. She spent a week on air looking like W. C. Fields and sounding like a foghorn. A thermos of sinfully decadent hot spiced toddy appeared along with a note in Claude's hand. "Drink up," it advised. "Even your sponsors can't top this. Who knows, it might even cure heartburn!"

So! Another reference to the medicinal items festooning "Ambrosia's" commercial spots. Via the same courier, Sophie fired the thermos back again, along with a fresh note stating that Sophie was quite capable of brewing up her own poison, thank you!

Too bad that CAM aired Sophie's special on mushrooms the next day, a show that had gone so well Sophie had finished the demonstration early and filled in the remaining moments with a cheerful little anecdote about gathering mushrooms in the spring, which she remembered wholesale from a European novel. Two hours later, when "Chez Claude" came on live, Claude skipped his final callers in order to face the camera gravely. For the first time, he mentioned "Ambrosia" directly.

"Please ignore Ms. Moore's advice about gathering mushrooms on your own," he told the thousands of surprised viewers. "The most innocent-looking fungi can be lethal, as," he smiled lopsidedly, "those of us know who have had experience with the ladies. Leave dicing with disaster to experts in the field."

"I didn't say people did it here!" Sophie spluttered, imagining people accusing her all over the city. "I said they did it in Europe!" Talk about overkill in getting back for the tart little note with the thermos!

Sophie mightn't have been so angry had not Claude struck on the heels of a visit to the newsroom where Sophie found a new assistant filling her old job and jokes about "Ambrosia" flying thick and fast. Sophie had stood on the edge of it all, only a visitor now, hopelessly out of date in the ever-changing whirlwind of hot local news and shattering world events. Fleeing back to Studio E, all Sophie could feel was her own life careening out of control. If she wasn't part of the newsroom any more, who was she? And if "Ambrosia" couldn't succeed—or at least be taken seriously—then was she nothing at all?

While she was gnawing her pencil over this, news reached her that Claude had appeared beside Jasmine Erle at a CXRT bash celebrating "Chez Claude." All right, Mr. Lacomte, Sophie said silently, there's still a few things yet you don't know about the media game! Once, just once, she was determined to taste the sweetness of scoring for her own side.

Sophie waited until Claude's next show, where he himself provided the opening by a comment about turning the most unpromising items into a gourmet's dream. Slipping a towel over the mouthpiece to disguise her voice, Sophie dialed, waited, and finally got through on air.

"In a world with so many going hungry, don't you think all possible sources of protein should be utilized?" she asked innocently. "Even those considered . . . um, less palatable?"

"Certainly!" Claude agreed. "There's plenty of ways to cure that little fault."

Ah, to slide so unsuspectingly into Sophie's trap!

"And don't you agree that a lot of very usable meat is wasted because of social prejudice? Horse meat, for instance."

"Horse meat is much in demand in France," Claude returned, without missing a beat. "No reason why it couldn't be made popular here."

Sophie thought of the horde of horse lovers already heading for their phones. A moment of pity swayed her—for Claude. Then she saw him smile meltingly at his guest, a marathon swimmer mad about sea vegetables and kelp.

"So other unusual meats, now wasted, could be popularized as food too?"

Claude paused at last, frowning.

"Depends on which kinds."

"Well, for instance, in the United States alone, thirteen million unwanted cats and dogs are destroyed every year. Wouldn't they be perfectly edible?"

"Edible certainly, but . . ."

"Ah ha! I knew you'd agree!" Sophie exclaimed, springing for the kill before Claude could realize what was hitting him. "Many societies have traditionally regarded dogs and cats as a food source. The Chinese, for instance, the Aztecs, and many North American native tribes kept dogs for food. Think how many people here could be given access to much-needed protein this way. Thank you for pointing out the feasibility of this hitherto overlooked resource now being wasted shamefully!"

Sophie hung with a click, leaving Claude spinning in the wind. Now, she thought, let's just see him say something to save himself from that!

Amazingly, Claude made no disclaimer at all. He merely smiled, shook his head, and went on to wrap up the show with never a suspicion of the avalanche awaiting.

All Sophie had expected to inflict had been a barrage of irate calls. She never dreamed of the riot of outraged animal lovers who pelted the front of CXRT with eggs and cat kibble, the mob that chased a CXRT news crew for seven panting blocks, the shrieking protesters who tore Claude's shirt nearly off his back when he tried to get to his car. The uproar made the second page of two of Toronto's newspapers. Finally, the Humane Society had to issue a public statement swearing that no pets currently in their shelters were going to be served up to the poor as stew.

CAM News had a picnic with the story which Sophie, ironically, had created but dared not take credit for. And, in the interview, Claude won her admiration. Despite bruises from the protesters, he refused to reject the idea of utilizing unwanted pets.

"In an ideal world, we'd all live on nectar and rose petals and no one would starve. But the caller was right. If we're going to eat animal protein, I fail to see the difference between calves, lambs, and puppies. From a strictly objective point of view, a large source of usable protein is being wasted because of public sentiment. The value of that sentiment, against real hunger, only the public can judge."

So Claude had his own brand of stubborn, perverse integrity despite the hole he knew he was digging himself into. Claude's profile had never been higher—a fact which suddenly pleased the Buckeroo mightily.

"Perfect timing for the fellow to kick up a storm," the dewlapped veteran informed Sophie. "He's just volunteered to come to 'Ambrosia' and do a joint show!''

Chapter Nine

Within just over a week, Claude was fitted into Sophie's schedule, though not fast enough to evade Lola Mallow. By her usual mysterious means, she managed to know instantly and hyped the meeting into something resembling a bullfight, with Claude the toreador, Sophie the easily provoked bull.

"They've already had a disagreement in front of CAM. How long, folks, until they stop using the knives on the vegetables and start using them on each other?"

The Buckeroo, deaf to Sophie's howls, regretted only that he was unable to raise the ad rates again, notice being much too short. Sophie came the nearest she had ever come to bolting from the show. Secretly, she quaked over the animal episode. And underneath everything, a renegade yearning to see Claude again defied her fiercest efforts to put him down. He must know I made that call, was all she could think. Now he's up to something of his own. I just know it! Agnes, as usual, was stuck with the task of calming her down.

"What you have to do, Soph, is take advantage of Claude's visit. He's the one with the skills, so just take up equal space in front of the camera and leave the work to him. The food is bound to be a resounding success and if you smile hard enough you can grab at least half the credit for yourself.

"And remember not to scowl," Agnes added, glancing at Sophie's face. "We don't want to give Lola any more

grist for her mill. Just smile and smile and keep up the
chatter. Show that Claude can do his worst and not get a
single rise out of you."

"But he's the most exasperating . . ."

Agnes tucked Nellie under her arm.

"Only if you think he is. Look, it's just mind over matter. We'll go over it together, every inch of the show. I'll
even write you some lines, if you want. We'll imagine
every possible thing Claude could say and have an answer
ready."

Unfortunately, Agnes hadn't the faintest suspicion about
Sophie's role in the saga of the fricasseed pound pooches.
Sophie would have liked to see her write a few lines to
deal with that! Morosely, Sophie stared into her tea, her
breathing short and sharp at the ordeal ahead. Agnes regarded Sophie soberly.

"Pardon me for saying so one more time," she commented, "but it sure looks to me as though you're hung up
on the guy!"

Instantly, Sophie's cheeks suffused darkly. "I am not!"
she coughed out before she could stop herself. "I . . ."

"I rest my case!" Agnes took a serene sip of tea.

"Oh no you don't. This is nothing but simple transferal.
You're the one who's hung up—on Sid! He must be nuts,
setting himself up for all those dreadful puns about the
weather!"

"It's your romantic life we're discussing. Ever since
Claude took you out to that restaurant, you've been sighing
like an engine and grinding your teeth at night. Why you
even . . ."

"Oh, and you're getting to be an expert on symptoms.
Well, Claude Lacomte is too full of himself to be interested.
You know very well I'm not going to let any man mess up
my plans. And I'm not going to be a . . . a darn trophy
either!"

This last cracked out with such force that Nellie jumped
for the sofa back. The words, the closest to an admission

Sophie had yet made, hung throbbing in the air between the two friends.

"Claude," Agnes pointed out quietly, "is not Stan Winterly."

"I don't want to talk about it!"

"Soph, I think you ought to . . ."

"I said, I didn't want to talk! Now let's sort out the show!"

Sophie had leaped up to pace the rug which would soon have a path down the middle. Whatever nerve Agnes had struck was too raw to be subjected to the scrutiny even of the closest of friends. A barrier had been thrown up and they both knew it. The subject of romance was closed between the two and remained closed through the weekend while they worked like horses over the show. Worked to the extent that Sophie marched into Studio E, feeling proof against a nuclear explosion.

Maybe even proof against Claude.

She arrived early, her brows knitted aggressively and wearing a dress that was the closest thing she owned to armor plate. The studio was in an uproar of preparation. Joel and Beth dashed frantically about trying to lay everything out as Claude had ordered it. Sophie herself had no intention of touching so much as a spoon today. Claude was the big expert. Let him work, leaving Sophie to hog the camera as much as she could manage.

However, as show time ticked inevitably closer, there was no sign of Claude at all. Sophie began to sweat in the palms of her hands. Where was he? If he didn't show, Sophie would have to somehow explain on camera and then deal with the complicated array of ingredients laid out before her. What if, for the second time, she got stuck with Claude's show!

Temper began to rise, accompanied by the awful thought that Claude might fail to appear deliberately—in revenge for the animal incident. But no, that was too unprofessional, impossible for Claude. Besides, he didn't know it had been her. He couldn't. Not when she'd been one among the dozens of anonymous callers Claude dealt with show after show. More likely was just stuck in traffic. Or . . . or had had an accident!

Cold anxiety crawled through her at the idea of Claude's Porsche in twisted pieces somewhere. He drove even more recklessly than she and Sophie was unable to shake the awful picture from her mind. Her palms grew damper while the back of her neck turned alternately hot, then cold. She began to watch the door, actually praying for Claude to arrive. What she got was Judy, the production assistant, rushing in with an armload of newspapers and her eyes half popping from her head.

"What's the matter?" Sophie demanded, pouncing on the girl. Judy exhibited a form of paralysis.

"Ah . . . you better look at the paper. Third section."

Sophie snatched the paper, trying to fathom how Claude's accident could have gotten into print so fast. The other papers were grabbed by the rest of the crew. Murray grinned back from Section C, photographed with the very same dinner Sophie had eaten with Claude at Mallory's. Next to the article was the entertainment column, where Lola described, ". . . a preview of Mallory's Valentine special, created to inspire romance in the coolest of bosoms. Chef Murray Bell's magic was tested, early in June, by none other than those famous TV personalities, Claude Lacomte and Sophie Moore, who slyly slipped into Mallory's together before their famous spat at CAM. The dinner certainly seems to have inspired emotion, for Claude was seen lavishing his attentions on Sophie's fair white arm. Do the sparks on the set mean banked fires underneath? Watch this space . . ."

Sophie flung the paper down, chest heaving.

"Photographs well, doesn't it," commented a husky voice at her shoulder. "Murray always did have a flair for color."

There stood Claude in his English tweeds and rangy impudence. Mindless joy lurched inside Sophie that he was safe, that he was alive, that he was lounging there with his hair windblown and his skin ruddy from the bracing outside air. Before her bounding heart could right itself, Sophie knew Claude had caught her reaction. A tendon jumped along his jaw and something emerald flared behind his lashes.

With that, Sophie's second reaction set in—agitation at her own emotions so foolishly out of control, fury at her own body for betraying her enough for Claude to see and be pleased, exasperation with Lola and the food editor who had ferreted out the trip to Mallory's. She stood immobile while Martin came crashing in, belatedly trying to be effective in his role.

"You're good and late, Claude. We don't have time for a run-through or anything. The crew's in a knot, the press is here, and the audience is packed to the doors! I hope you know what you're doing!"

"Oh, I do," Claude replied in a voice smooth as fine aged whiskey. Sophie saw that he meant to carry on here exactly as he did on his own show—and the dangerous flash in her eye conveyed that she was having none of it.

"Murray's supposed to be your friend," she shot out as they stood apart at the side, waiting to go on. "Didn't you tell him to keep quiet?"

"I haven't spoken to Murray since that evening at Mallory's. What he says to newspapers is entirely his own affair."

"Well it's our affair now!"

"Do we have an affair, Sophie?"

The words curled round her, teasing and perilous.

"If we do, I'm the last to know about it," she shot back. "Now let's get this thing over with so all those people out there can put their eyeballs back in their skulls and get on with life!"

Being thoroughly rattled, was not a good state in which to go on air—especially to make her debut on live television, which the Buckeroo had insisted upon for this episode. Newspapers rustled all over the audience which stared with eyes big as teacups. Even the Buckeroo was there, obviously hoping for carnage. Yet even as Max gave the five-second countdown, Sophie rallied. This was her show, her set, her studio. Claude wasn't going to hypnotize her into compliance while he took over. If it was the last thing she did alive, she meant to keep control of "Ambrosia." At the signal, she strolled out, smile fixed in cement while Claude followed, eliciting wild applause from the spectators. Sophie smiled wider, cheeks tight. When Claude waited for her to take her place beside him she got in her first move.

"Oh, you're the expert here, Claude," she said sweetly. "I think I'll just watch and let you handle everything!"

Despite Claude's glance of surprise, Max's signals, and Martin's furious grimaces, Sophie remained unmoved. The only way to prevent Claude from toying with her on the set was not to participate at all. Then everyone would see just who was going to play with whom.

Claude shrugged and began—and almost instantly, Sophie wondered whether she hadn't made a mistake after all. Claude moved into the action so smoothly as to make Sophie seem quite superfluous. She felt all attention focusing on him no matter how much she attempted to sidle in front of Camera One.

"So tell me, Sophie," Claude asked genially as he set oil to sizzling in the bottom of a pan, "now that you've been with 'Ambrosia' for some time now, do you plan to make your future in the fascinating new world of haute cuisine?"

So that was his plan, Sophie decided, even as the audience tittered. He meant to treat her the way he treated the guests on his own show. She forced her smile to stay in place.

"That depends," was the only thing neutral she could think of to say.

"Depends on what?"

He wasn't going to let her off any hook. Sophie watched his fingers skillfully chop celery into symmetrical pieces. She wished now she was in possession of that knife.

On whether I ever get to make an omelette boil, she wanted to say, but found herself muttering something so lame, sweat started up on her forehead. Why did she have the feeling that Claude knew every time her dress fabric brushed across her skin?

"Tell us about the restaurant," somebody from the audience shouted—and the melee was on.

At first, Sophie could only watch speechlessly. She never took questions from the audience or had them participate other than to provide applause. Now, once Claude started it, there was no way anyone was going to get the barrage to stop.

"Have you asked Sophie out since?"

"Did she really knock that set over deliberately?"

"Are you going to date Jasmine Erle?"

Claude fielded everything with the ease of a big league player catching fly balls, never once pausing with what he was doing at the counter. He tossed several of the balls to Sophie who, had she actually been one of his guests, would have used the opportunity to laugh and tease and turn the conversation flatteringly to herself.

But she wasn't one of Claude's guests. She was supposed to be the host here—and the subject everyone was playing with was far too sensitive to be bandied about like a Frisbee in the park.

Gamely, she began to fight to get control back, smiling so wide her face hurt while ignoring all the hands waving eagerly in the audience to get her attention.

"That's compote of duck you're making," she purred, casually tasting Claude's sauce. "Fifteen hundred calories a serving and most of them from fat. How are your admirers going to keep their slim waists if you encourage them to eat things like that?"

The strong lights overhead illuminated Claude with uncompromising clarity. Sophie could see the supple muscles moving as he worked, pick out a hidden scar—surely a hockey scar—in his eyebrow, sense the tang of pine that always conjured such green forests in her mind. He quirked her a look with such confident magnetism she felt the physical pull. But she could not forget he had already seen naked tumult in her eye.

"Perhaps the only admirer I'm interested in has a slim waist even if she fills up on rusty nails and boiled construction boots." He paused long enough to let this direct quote from the lunch at Rita's bloom in Sophie's mind. Two brilliant flags of color flared in her cheeks. This was typical! Typical of the sniping that had been going on for weeks. Infuriated, she saw Claude measure the effect of this dart before turning to the audience. "For the mighty hunters among you," he went on, "a fine compote can also be made out of rabbit."

"Or cats!" Sophie added, remembering the fraudulent Parisian restaurant Agnes had once told her about.

The effect was instant, shattering silence, making Sophie realize what she had just said. The devil made me do it, she wanted to shout. But of course, she could only stand there and watch as Claude slowly set down a ceramic bowl and walked around the end of the counter, completely oblivious to the fact that he was off the set for both Camera One and Camera Two. Mardi Gras scarlet was working its way up from his collar, making him yank his constricting tie knot loose.

"You!" he roared at the top of his lungs. "You did that to me about the animals! You made that call!"

Sophie gulped incriminatingly, not in the least comforted now by the idea that, had she just kept her mouth shut, Claude really would never ever have known.

Chapter Ten

After this finish, Studio E emptied speedily as a picnic ground in a hailstorm, the audience melting through the side doors, the crew scattering out of range. Claude shrugged on his jacket, settling it hard on his shoulders. He'd lost it on air and he knew he'd lost it and his face remained darkly suffused with color.

"Where's my briefcase?" he demanded stiffly of Sophie, the only live human left.

"In the pantry!" Then, wanting any excuse to escape the tension popping like firecrackers between them, "I'll get it."

The pantry, at the extremity of the back corridor, was actually a hastily converted supply closet still reeking of solvent. Sophie marched to the narrow, high-ceilinged room, just reaching for the case when footsteps echoed behind her. Claude was following her in, making room for himself by shifting the chair propped under the doorknob.

"Don't close that door!" Sophie barked—too late. The door shut with a firm and final *snick*.

"Why not? Afraid to get too close for comfort?"

"Handle broke last week. Can't be opened from the inside."

Claude swung round and jerked at the knob. True to Sophie's word, the door held fast. Claude banged on it with the flat of his hand, then shouted.

"Won't do you a bit of good," Sophie commented.

143

"Beth and Joel have streaked for the donut shop by now. This wing'll be empty as a church until morning."

"The night watchman . . ."

"Sleeps in the lobby until the robins wake him up. We're stuck till the staff comes in at eight—unless you want to try tunneling."

Was that outright panic on Claude's face, Sophie wondered as he looked around at the shelves of supplies and utensils, the untidy heap of disused props, the old pop crate Sophie stood on to reach what she wanted. Never had his elegance looked more out of place, never had his masculinity so filled an enclosed space.

"Till tomorrow?" he asked incredulously.

"Tomorrow!"

Immediately, Sophie took possession of the open space where the shelves did not take up the wall. Claude emitted a frustrated growl, thumping his fist one last time against the door.

"Maybe if you fling yourself against it, the hinges will give way," Sophie put in tartly. "Then you can get busy rounding up another swooning guest for your show."

For a moment, Claude looked as though he might try it. He shot Sophie a scathing look.

"I don't have to round up guests. I have to beat them away with a stick!"

Sophie let out a yip of laughter.

"Lola is right. Certainly nothing wrong with your ego!"

"Ego, my dear," Claude drawled, "is how you get places in this world. It's otherwise known as healthy self-esteem—something I doubt can be discussed with you after the fiascos you put on with such touching regularity."

He stalked over to the flour bins and stood outlined grandly. The single ceiling bulb shed yellow light upon his cheekbones and illuminated the dust motes swirling around his feet like mini clouds of glory.

"After today, I guess you can join the club."

Claude's racing flush made Sophie regret her rash words. Why was she compelled to prod and poke, the knot of emotion inside demanding she get a reaction, any reaction out of him? Anything but indifference. Claude moved as though to retort, but caught himself. Sophie's eyes lingered on his hair a second before she could pull her gaze away. Claude scanned the shelves as though they might yield an axe to do in the door.

Sophie's nerves snapped and quivered, for Claude was altogether too large and too near. His presence filled the tiny room like a crackling hum, an overload of the electricity that had jumped about Sophie's system since he appeared in the studio. Silence was far worse than verbal warfare, for it threw into raw relief the crazy, unadmitted hope she'd harbored for the meeting today. A hope gone up in smoke on the set. Oh, she needed something—anything—to calm herself. Next to her, at eye level, stood a fat bottle of cooking sherry.

"Driven to tipple in secret?" Claude inquired, following her line of vision.

"Certainly not! I do it in the open if I want."

Just to show him, she unscrewed the cap impulsively and poured a slosh into a cracked Snoopy mug. Claude's hand shot out.

"Just like you to drink wine from a cup. Here." He found a glass goblet, dumped the contents of the mug into it and handed it to Sophie. "If you're going to get into the cooking sherry, at least do it with a bit of style!"

"Style it is," she flung back, tickled by his disapproving glare. "Here's to the depths of depravity!" Her defiant gulp turned out to be deliciously sweet—exactly Sophie's idea of what a wine should be. Since Claude continued to scowl, Sophie poured more sherry into the cup he had relieved her of and held it out.

"Might as well join me as stand there like a fence post. Going to be a long night. Unless, of course, there's nothing left of us in the morning but bits of stuffing."

To her surprise, he accepted the cup. Sophie took a second gulp and felt the stuff burn a trail down to a stomach that had had nothing but dabs and tastes all day. Claude regarded her sherry-moistened mouth, then took a sharp, quick swallow himself.

"I still say it was a low blow, that call about the cats and dogs!"

"Wasn't it, though!" Sophie agreed, wary lest Claude wanted to continue the quarrel, but pleased with her own resourcefulness despite the enormous brouhaha resulting. "There are still tons of ideas you haven't heard of yet."

"And you intend to try them all!"

"If I have to!" The sherry now enabled Sophie to regard Claude levelly over her goblet. "In sheer self-defense."

"I'm not the one who started this."

"And I'm not the one who hasn't been able to get over a fit of pique about losing control of a show."

"I merely refused to have my standards compromised— no matter with whom!"

His gaze slid so hotly over Sophie that she had to gulp more sherry as fortification.

"My, aren't we convivial when we want to be," she shot back.

Now Claude grinned slightly, like a smiling lynx.

"Despite your weakness for warfare, your barbs will do you no good in here. Not a single mike is on."

His hair tumbled distractingly across his forehead and the ruddy, tanned health of his skin glowed under the bulb.

"If you didn't want to do battle, why did you agree to guest on 'Ambrosia'?"

Claude remained silent for a very long time, his jaw working slightly. Then he heaved a sigh and shifted against the door.

"Did it ever occur to you," he said slowly, "that I agreed because maybe there didn't seem to be any other way I was going to get to see you?"

Sophie's breath came loose and she gaped openly at him. "Why?" she asked, so taken aback by what he had said that she sounded completely blank.

"I can't imagine!" Claude returned drily. "Why do

bears knock over beehives? Why do cattle eat windfall apples and fall over drunk?''

Oh, he was baiting her again. And she, fool that she was, had just suffered a jolt of adrenaline nearly strong enough to separate her ankles from her feet. Shakily, she poured herself another shot of sherry and felt her stomach growl. Suddenly, and not surprisingly, she was ravenously hungry. Emotion always had that effect. And besides, it had been ages since her body had had any fuel. She turned crankily away.

"I'm starving, you know. I've had neither lunch nor dinner.''

The large refrigerator, that might have yielded something edible, stood outside on the edge of the set. The shelves here bore all sorts of staples, but nothing that could be eaten in its raw state. On top of hunger, Sophie's feet hurt and she needed to sit down. This meant the floor, which, luckily, the janitor seemed to have swabbed out sometime in the last three months. She sank down with a sigh and drew her knees up. The change in perspective made Claude look enormous, even forbidding, the whole underside of his face thrown into shadow by the dangling bulb.

"Might as well join me," she told him, "unless you'd prefer to stand against the wall all night.''

"Lucky for us you're a sucker when you go out to shop.''

Stacked in a corner were three enormous sacks of rice which Sophie had got talked into, her first exploratory trip to Kensington Market. Now she knew she could make casseroles for fifty years and not deplete them. Claude tugged them longways against the wall where they made quite a creditable couch.

"The original beanbag chair. Try it.''

Folding his long frame down, Claude settled comfortably. After a moment's hesitation, Sophie plopped down too, the sherry making her relax, adding a swirl of rose to her creamy cheeks, and allowing her to regard Claude more directly.

"I don't suppose the great chef could toss together anything edible in here?"

This time Claude actually laughed. It had been a long time since Sophie had heard that thrilling sound, and it occurred to her how much, how very much, she had missed it.

"Wonders are my specialty. Miracles I cannot do."

He tossed back yet more of the cooking sherry. Sophie sat silently for a while, then jumped bolt upright.

"We don't have to starve! I laid in essential stores as soon as the Buckeroo stuck me with this job! Give me a boost!"

After Sophie hopped ineffectually toward the top shelf, Claude grasped her about the knees, lifting her easily. The sudden physical contact flung into her mind what a night locked up with Claude could really mean. Sophie swayed, recovered, and stretched to retrieve the precious box from behind a stockpot. Claude lowered her slowly and let go of her even more slowly.

"What do you have?" he asked, his breath slightly ragged.

"Uh . . ." Sophie struggled to remember even as the oh-so-familiar label floated before her face. "Galaxy Cakes. A whole box of them. My favorite!"

Claude stared, then gingerly turned one over.

"How long have these been here?"

"Oh, from about the week after you hurt your arm. In the newsroom, you learn to keep stashes. I clean forgot about this one till now. Lucky, eh?"

Sophie began tearing the wrapper off one cake which emerged in its semicircle shape, its chocolate as dark, its filling as frothy and gooey as if it had just come off the assembly line.

"You don't intend to eat that?"

"I sure do." Sophie took an enormous bite. "Pure heaven!"

"But they're . . ." Claude swiftly counted the weeks on his fingers, ". . . ancient! They could make you sick!"

Sophie shook her head. "No way. I've had them a lot older than this. They never go stale. Like they're magic or something."

"You mean they're so full of preservatives they could stay fresh in an Egyptian tomb!"

"Wonders of modern science!" Sophie set the box between herself and Claude. "Help yourself. Plenty for us both!"

Claude remained silent, staring at Sophie until she realized he was fascinated by a flick of icing on her chin. A quiver passed through her as she quickly licked it away. At the same time, the sugar from the Galaxy Cakes hit her system, mellowing her the way nicotine calmed smokers and caffeine smoothed out coffee addicts. Claude sat down on the rice sack again, his legs crossed in front of him. He had now shed his jacket and was flexing his shoulders against the wall, a bare foot or two of space between himself and Sophie.

"So," Claude said without warning, "when are you going to quit trying to cook and go back to the newsroom where you belong?"

Sophie tensed, ready to defend her show hotly, especially against Claude, whose barbs could be merciless. However, with the cooking sherry beginning to circulate nicely in her system, argument began to look futile.

"I miss the newsroom," she admitted. "Believe me, I've begged and pleaded, but nothing has any effect on the Buckeroo."

"If you really hate it so much, why don't you just quit?"

Claude reached for his sherry, grimacing, but also taking a long sip. There was that tone in his voice again, male confidence, a man who spoke from a position of wealth and achievement and didn't understand that one couldn't just stroll out and take whatever one wanted. Sophie bristled.

"Look, I'm not suicidal. If I walked out, I'd never get another job in television—ever. I'm not a big celebrity," she said with edge, "who can afford to have fits of temper."

"Lola Mallow thinks you are."

"Lola Mallow," Sophie shot back, "has caused more trouble than a pack of hyenas on the prowl!"

Claude emitted what sounded like an involuntary creak of mirth. Instantly, Sophie grew aware of the soft rustle of fabric as he moved, even the shifting of the rice beneath him. Her brows knitted as she finished the Galaxy Cake.

"Sure has." Claude agreed quite amiably. "Have you ever wondered where she gets her information?"

"Spies! Anybody in her position has to have an amazing espionage network. She set us up as an item way back that time with the fire hose. Really, you can't trust anybody."

"Can't you?"

So much permeating Claude's simple response! Sophie felt him shift closer and began to wonder what their war had been all about. The sherry was making Sophie faintly light-headed—and acting rather like a truth serum, breaking down inner barriers, inundating her with the knowledge that she had been thinking about Claude, dreaming about him, hardly able to get him out of her mind for a second. Almost as if . . . as if . . .

As if she were definitively nuts about the guy!

The shock of the thought caused Sophie to hiccup involuntarily, catching some sherry on the way down. Claude thumped her expertly between the shoulder blades.

"What was that all about?"

"G . . . gas! Sherry got in the wrong way!"

A little more and Claude might have had to apply the Heimlich maneuver. Sophie found she was tempted. Beside her, Claude was actually helping himself to some more sherry. The bottle sat on the floor between them, dusty in the glaring light.

"CXRT has been hinting about a new job for me," Claude said with rather elaborate casualness. "My own talk show."

"What!"

Sophie immediately forgot her cataclysmic suspicions of the moment before. Talk show host was an unimaginable leap up the scale, putting Claude in there with Oprah and Leno and turning him into a really major force overnight. Sophie, after her anchorwoman stint, had sneaking ambitions in that direction herself. How did the man do it!

"Seems they're impressed with the attention a mere food show has got. They think I could really do well with something big!"

"But you haven't got the kind of background . . . I mean, a talk show covers such a broad range of topics. You have to be . . ."

Sophie faltered, determined not to sound envious. Claude hitched toward her, grinning like a brigand.

"Hey, how much can I need?" he murmured, one finger reaching out to tap her under the chin, "I've got a brain and I've got sex appeal. You yourself said that. Except about the brain, of course."

Sophie would have given up a month of holidays for a snappy reply, but none was forthcoming. She relapsed into silence, noting that the light outside the heavily wired window was fading and the naked bulb above their heads growing more harsh. She knew the streetlights would be coming on and, as if in tune with her thought, a small sharp crack sounded, plunging the pantry into dimness.

"Now the bulb's gone!"

"Too bright anyway," Claude said complacently.

Renewed silence hung thick for a while, and then there was a suspicious rattle of plastic. Claude was helping himself to a Galaxy Cake. Sophie listened to him eat and said nothing until the cake was gone.

"How was it?"

"Matches the sherry."

Heavy irony didn't prevent him from serving himself yet again from the bottle, tipping it to get the last drop. Sophie hadn't realized they were putting away so much. Luckily there were more bottles where that one had come from.

"I know you think I'm frivolous," Claude began out of the blue, "and you're the crusader here. Well how about this! How about world peace through food!"

That had to be one of his jokes, but Sophie was far enough gone to mull his proposal over half seriously.

"Well, the world certainly needs more food, with the population exploding the way it is, doubling and tripling way past anything the planet can support. We just can't seem to make people stop reproducing."

"Perhaps it's because of this." Claude nuzzled Sophie's neck. "It's just so appealing."

Sophie pulled away with a jump of nerves. Who did he think he was coming on to!

"You know what I mean. People could have all the sex they wanted—if they just used proper birth control."

"I bet Nellie McClung would do a number on that." Claude chuckled into her ear.

He sounded altogether too flip, which stirred Sophie up. She was having no one treat her heroine lightly. Not to mention the totally terrifying overpopulation problem.

"You bet she would. If Nellie were around, every last woman in the world would get to decide how many babies she wanted or if she even wanted any at all. No woman willingly has children she knows she cannot feed. . . ."

"Which," Claude murmured, nibbling now at her ear, "brings us back to topic one. World peace through food. Or rather, through nutrition. Your strong point," he added ironically.

Sophie remained unspeaking, determined not to rise to that one. She also didn't move her ear. Claude laughed softly and went on.

"Badly fed people are unhappy people, and that's just as true in the overfed west as in the underfed other parts of the world. A person living on grease, sugar, and junk is hostile, aggressive, paranoid and very short on attention span."

"Sounds like the emperor Nero!"

"My point exactly. He probably had lead poisoning. The Romans used lead as a sweetener in their sauces, you know."

Before Sophie could croak, Claude grew more expansive.

"Think of it, Sophie. Who causes wars? Aggressive, hostile, paranoid people who can't think straight. Who beats up women, abuses children, fights with neighbors and turns to drugs and alcohol for relief? Same as above. Etcetera!''

"Oh, and you'd have them all on salads and aerobics!''

"I would if I could. Actually,'' Claude paused as though thinking about whether to expose an inmost thought or not, "I've been thinking about doing something. Forming an institute, say, to promote efficient use of food resources. After I meet crusaders,'' Sophie could actually feel him smiling in the dark, "I can't help but get altruistic urges like that.''

He was very close again, his shoulder warm against Sophie's. She wondered if perhaps, just perhaps, she had underestimated him. When she didn't move away, Claude insinuated himself even more comfortably on the bags of rice. "Sometimes I wonder,'' he said, "just what we've been scrapping about.''

"Don't you know?''

"No. What is it?''

The two dozen items on the tip of Sophie's tongue all vanished. She frowned, her mind throwing up only a hazy blank.

"I don't know. Mushrooms? Trivialities?''

Somehow, she couldn't tell how, Claude's arm was resting across her shoulder and she was leaning against his ribs. It was wonderful how well she fitted there.

Claude drew a long breath which Sophie could feel fluttering the hair at her temple. A delicious tingle, all unbidden, tracked down her spine. Vaguely, some voice told her this was known as consorting with the enemy, but she couldn't bring herself to care. Claude felt exclusively hers again, and who was she to disturb the sensation?

"Fighting over trivialities is said to be a sign,'' Claude breathed.

"Of what? Reduced intelligence?''

Sophie heard a giggle ending in a hiccup—her own. She clapped her hand over her mouth, amazed at the sound.

"Yes. Or else," he rumbled quietly, "the trivialities are merely a symptom, a mask for a much deeper issue."

The sherry fumes vanished away and Sophie felt her stomach contract. Anxiety made her unsure whether she wanted to hear any more of this.

"In our case, I think it's definitely reduced intelligence," she put in lightly, glad the ceiling light was off.

Claude remained unspeaking for so long that Sophie was suddenly, irrationally afraid he agreed with her.

"I think not," he said finally, releasing breath as though the words carried some extraordinary weight.

The very last light of day faded and Sophie could look out of the high upper section of the window, which was not frosted, and see the three-quarter moon shining. The window faced the parking lot, so no streetlights cut jarringly into the gloom—only the moonlight, turned into a dappled, lacy tracery by the wild sumacs thrusting their way up along the outside wall.

Sophie felt her heart racing and slowing, and pumping erratically as whatever Claude had raised hung in the air between them. She became vitally aware of Claude, the rise and fall of his ribs against her, the easy set of his arm, the strange languor that was taking possession of her limbs. Nothing like this had happened to her, even with Stan.

"You know," Claude admitted appreciatively, "that trick you pulled on me about the animals—it was pretty clever."

"You think so?"

"Between you, me, and the gatepost, yes. Brilliant, actually—though it took me a while to appreciate the wit."

Claude's head leaned back and he chuckled softly, with no trace of his previous anger. Sophie basked unconscionably in this unexpected praise—especially when he admitted that all the furor was what had got him thinking about food uses.

"You take your job very seriously, don't you?" he went on. "I mean the one in the newsroom."

"Oh, if I could only get back to it . . ." Longing laced Sophie's words, and she sighed heavily.

"Instead of being a star in your own right."

"I told you, I didn't ask for it, I didn't want it, I did everything I could think of to get out of it. Everybody in the world knows I'll never be able to cook."

"That's why they adore you!"

"Adore to laugh at me!" Sophie amended astringently.

"No, adore you. Don't you understand? People love those who honestly reflect back their own humanity. That's what you do every time you try so hard and still screw up a basic casserole on your show."

"Look, you don't have to make up a whole load of tripe just because we're locked up together," Sophie bit out, highly defensive on this sensitive topic. "I suppose the audience adores you for the way you manage to be one walking seduction machine with all those lovely guests."

Laughter spurted out of Claude.

"All of us have our cross to bear. Can I help it if I'm catnip to the ladies? You turned me on to the fact."

"Me!"

"That time you came over to my apartment. Your little lecture gave me the whole idea for my new show. That's what I love about you. Every time I run into you, you end up changing the course of my life!"

Love about you!

Sophie's heart went racketing madly against her sternum. No, it was just a figure of speech. People used it a dozen times a day—about jogging shoes and puppies and . . . tuna fish. And suppose Claude did love her—it would be nothing but a fling until he moved on to his next interest. He was just that kind of man. A sensualist, a hedonist. Sophie had nothing whatever against hedonists, glorious creatures enjoying the sun. But she had foresight and goals. A fling with a man like Claude might leave her sadly wrecked on the beach.

These thoughts raced erratically through her mind even as she felt Claude drawing her closer, nuzzling her hair. It felt so wonderful. She found herself powerless to move.

"So tell me all about the man who turned you off romance."

A sneak attack on a topic Sophie hadn't touched in ages.

"It's ancient history."

"Not to me."

Claude's arms were around her, the way Stan's arms had been around her. Funny how she felt cherished instead of trapped the way Stan had made her feel.

"He was a mining engineer doing graduate work while I was finishing my degree in political science. I got swept away, I'm afraid—by Stan and college radio at the same time. Radio. I spent hours spilling it all to Stan, making plans, dreaming. Quite over the moon, I'm afraid."

"In love?"

"Oh yes!" Sophie still cringed to remember the ecstasies she'd felt when Stan was around. "Then everything blew up."

"How?" Claude found the sensitive spot at the corner of her jaw, almost making Sophie forget what she was saying.

"Graduation came. I'd managed acceptance into a journalism school—and believe me I really had to fight for it. Had a job lined up to help pay for it, everything."

Sophie needed a prompt from Claude in the form of a nip on the neck. With a heave of her bosom, she ploughed on.

"The night of our graduation dance, Stan announced he'd taken a job in this godforsaken mining camp way up on James Bay and that he'd also got the marriage license and reserved married living quarters for us. We'd be leaving, he said, for the wilderness at the end of the month. I'd been talking to him for six months and he hadn't heard a word I'd said. I'd been completely invisible to him. It was the wierdest feeling. I'll never forget sitting on the frat house terrace trying to absorb the shock."

"I have a hard time imagining someone as forceful as you putting up with a fellow like that."

Sophie grinned ruefully into the gloom.

"Well, to put it baldly, he was gorgeous. My hormones ran away with me. I swore never to let it happen again!"

"And has it?"

Sophie felt lips, light as a butterfly's wing, brush the side of her neck. A terrible longing, all mixed up with fear, took hold of her. She tried to pull away, the wounds of the past very fresh now in her mind. Claude held her firmly.

"I'm not Stan," he murmured against her ear. "I haven't the faintest intention of whisking you off to James Bay."

His arms were fully around her now, lifting her against him. The scent of pine came to her, conjuring from the sumac shadows a whispering northern forest. Sophie tried to resist, but Claude was now kissing her eyelids, filling her with a liquid tenderness that spilled through her limbs and drew her breath out in a whispering sigh. The sherry had blurred the edges of reality so that she could give herself up to Claude's caresses without thinking, without, for once, arguing with herself. She kissed him back ever so slowly, even as the sherry claimed her and she nestled down into the sweet cocoon of sleep.

Chapter Eleven

Slowly, very slowly, Sophie bobbed toward wakefulness through a rainbow haze. Murmuring, she snuggled tighter against the warm body next to her. An arm encircled her shoulders, drawing her protectively into its shelter. Under her cheek, a broad chest rose and fell in deep, rhythmic breathing. Never before had Sophie felt so cozy and so cherished.

This stage lasted until the pounding inside Sophie's head, the weights on her eyelids, the grittiness in her mouth intruded. She forced her lids open. Dust motes rose lazily from the floor, turned into spangled gold by the sunlight spilling through the narrow window. Sophie swallowed hard, trying to orient herself. The glorious warmth that enveloped her was human arms—male arms. As was the chest she nestled against.

It was morning—and she was lying entwined in the arms of Claude Lacomte!

Woozily, Sophie extricated herself, supported on one wobbly elbow. The hammer in her head turned into a pneumatic drill and the room swayed around her. Two empty bottles labeled cooking sherry lay on the floor on their sides.

Hangover! Sophie thought. She hadn't had such a lulu since she'd gone, innocent as a kitten, to that Monster Mash frat party in her freshman year.

Her eyes focused on Claude. He did indeed look entrancing, sound asleep against the plump rice sacks. His amber hair, touched by a shaft of sunlight, lay rich as fine Provençal honey across his forehead. His lashes gleamed. His lips were tempting and unguarded and so very near. Despite the hangover, Sophie felt a heat spilling through her. She could not exactly remember last night, but she knew in her bones that much had been said and much understood. It would come back to her. In the meantime . . .

In the meantime, a doorway slammed. The station was coming to life. Any moment, the pantry door might open and . . .

And the whole world would discover the ''Ambrosia'' star clutched in the arms of her archrival, Claude Lacomte!

Sophie shot bolt upright, appalled! She must get out! And she must get Claude out. Oh, she would simply die if it got out that she had spent the night alone with Claude, obviously drinking and nestled in the same warm nest of rice sacks.

Her movements began to rouse Claude. He stirred, reaching for Sophie, causing her, in spite of all, to pause. Oh, he was a handsome devil, laying flushed and undefended in sleep. Desire tugged at Sophie's innards, the desire to spend just one more moment looking at the man beside her. Yet the crack of a distant voice galvanized her. She had to make good her escape.

In the same instant, Claude came fully awake. He half sat up, his face mirroring Sophie's—sleepy, hungover, full of sweet recollections, and not exactly sure what had hit him.

''What's the matter?'' he asked, rubbing his eyes.

''What's the matter! It's morning. People are coming in. Any time now, they're going to find us in here together!''

To Claude's credit, it took him a full thirty seconds to comprehend what Sophie was so alarmed about.

''So?''

''Good grief! If we're found here together, Lola will have us for breakfast, grilled over charcoal!''

Sophie was now infinitely relieved to see they both still had their clothes on. Whatever had happened last night, it hadn't progressed past the point of no return. Claude must have read this thought, so clearly illustrated on her face.

"Would you really hate to be found with me that much?"

When in a panic, Sophie was not at her most sweet-tempered, or her most logical. No plans to whisk her to James Bay, he had said. Or anywhere else, probably—except into his bed. A whole parade of lovelies formed in her mind—with herself as last in the line.

"Oh, it's fine for you. Ho ho ho! Just one more conquest, one more notch in the great Claude Lacomte's belt. All the funnier if it happens to be Sophie Moore. Well, not on your life, buster. Not here! Not now!"

"Sophie, you're going off the deep end . . ."

"Look, I don't have time to quibble. We have to get out!"

Claude surveyed the rice sacks, still bearing the marks of their bodies, and then at Sophie's stark face. His own expression closed and stiffened, watching Sophie as she skittered round the tiny space, searching for escape with the same fruitless results as the evening before.

Trapped! They were trapped and there was to be no help until someone opened the door, exposing a night of obvious debauchery for the entire world to see. Frantically, Sophie shook the wire window grille, her fingers sliding up and stopping suddenly at the top.

"Look! It's only held by two screws here. If we can get them out, the window might slide up enough to let us out."

Snatching up a knife from the cutlery bin, Sophie attacked the screws, laboriously trying to prize them out of their rusted-in, painted-on bed.

"Here, give me that if you want to get away so badly!"

He needn't swear so much under his breath, Sophie thought, as Claude went to work. A fine sweat was breaking out on her forehead. She could definitely hear steps in the corridors now and voices raised in greeting.

"There!"

The second small screw bounced to the floor. Bracing

his feet, Claude worked at the grille until it yielded with a *scree* and slid upward.

Sophie's heart did a great bounce of relief. Just one bounce, since the stubborn grille rose only a few inches and stuck fast. No one, short of Hercules, was going to get it past the warped, swelled section of wooden window frame.

Claude opened the window behind the grille and swore again, this time more colorfully than Sophie had yet heard. She realized there was no way Claude was ever going to lever his big body through the narrow slot now open to the outside.

"I can get through," Sophie volunteered swiftly. "Then I'll come open the pantry door and get you out the back."

"The back?"

"The delivery entrance. If you're fast and keep your head down, you can be away before anybody knows the difference!"

Turning her head to the side, Sophie wedged herself under the grille and pushed until her shoulders squeezed through and she got half her body out. Unfortunately, her hips jammed, leaving her hanging down over the sill, her face a foot from a scraggly flower bed. Since her feet were off the ground, she would have hung there, helpless and seething, had she been alone.

"Wriggle," Claude ordered, pushing hard from inside.

"I can't!" Sophie flailed for something to grab onto.

Nevertheless, with a sudden jerk, her torso slid through and Sophie collapsed into the petunias below. However, the sound of the Buckeroo's Jeep brought her to her feet in a running roll. She escaped around the corner, just as the boss pulled into the lot.

"Morning, Miss Moore."

Only when Andrea at the front desk gave Sophie a startled look did Sophie realize her hair must be standing on end from her night's adventure, and that her dress was an unholy mess from the petunia bed.

Distracted, she sped along the halls, running her fingers

through her hair and brushing at her clothes. As she approached the region of Studio E, she had to dodge staff and once duck into a washroom for five heart-thudding minutes. She not only had to get Claude out, she had to get him out unseen. Oh, pray that no one would be making a delivery at this early hour.

She arrived at the pantry, unnoticed—but, alas, too late!

The door stood open and a hubbub of excited spectators had already built up. Flattening herself behind an electrical box, Sophie caught sight of Claude transfixed by a dozen pairs of avid eyes. His jacket still lay crumpled on the rice sacks. His hair, like Sophie's, stood uncombed and his face was traced with the night's activities.

In disaster, it was said, everything goes into slow motion. Sophie knew from personal experience that this was only too true. This moment proved to be the slowest motion she had ever lived through. She saw Claude lift his hand to his head, face the discovering knot of people as one would face a small pack of wolves, and make an enormous effort to pull himself together. A chorus of voices rose up.

"Claude! Why are you in the pantry?"

"We thought you went home . . ."

"Sophie was supposed to . . ."

"Where's Sophie anyway? She was coming in early today . . ."

Sophie saw people actually begin to look around, as though for her. No one spotted her save Claude, whose green gaze swiftly picked out her form in the shadows. The look in Claude's eyes made Sophie quail. And he had a right to be furious with her for failing to pull off his rescue in time to avoid this scene.

And, somewhere, there's a spy among us, Sophie thought. There's no way Lola is not going to find out about this!

"Claude! What are you doing still here! You look like something the cat dragged in from a ditch!"

The booming question brought in its wake Martin Scorley and, oh horrors, the Buckeroo. Dry-mouthed, Sophie crammed herself further back as they passed, knowing that, wearing her disheveled dress from the day before, there was no way she could plausibly explain her presence if she were found on the scene. The situation was beyond help. There was nothing to do but abandon ship as quickly as possible.

She could not, however, go anywhere until the pantry cleared—and Claude answered the Buckeroo's question.

In fascinated horror, Sophie watched the chase of expressions on Claude's face. She was beginning to realize how drastic some of the things she had said to him were and sincerely wished she could retract them. However, retraction was out of the question. Right now, she only wanted escape.

"Enough!! Claude," the Buckeroo demanded loudly, advancing his bulk into the pantry, "I want to know what's going on!"

For just a moment, Claude was so still that Sophie wondered whether the hangover had short-circuited his thought processes. Then he tore a hand through his hair, shook himself, and grabbed for his jacket.

"I . . . guess I got ill," he rasped out finally, managing to look shaky on his feet. "Came on all of a sudden. Dropped me right here where I stood when I came to get my briefcase!"

"Meet me," the voice grated over the phone, "in the Allen Gardens greenhouse right away!"

Sophie's blood pressure lurched skyward. The voice was Claude's, and Sophie frayed beyond endurance.

"I wouldn't go to the door if you were hung on it!" she cried in a passion. "Not after the day I've put in because of you!"

"You'd better meet me. That is if you want to get into your apartment again or start your car. I have your purse!"

Her purse!

She'd been frantic all day about her purse, supposing it still to be in the pantry just lying there for someone else to find and start asking questions. Claude must have smuggled it out under his jacket.

"All right, I'll be there," she replied shortly, after a hard internal struggle. "Twenty minutes." Then, with just a flick of her old self, "You better be wearing a disguise!"

After Claude's incredible statement that morning, Sophie had fled again, this time to her office, meaning only to snatch her purse and speed on home. That's when she remembered taking her purse to the pantry—and almost had hysterics on the spot.

Only she hadn't had time for hysterics. She had to gather the remnants of her resourcefulness and take what action she could. First, a change of clothes! Sophie flung open her cupboard in desperate hope and found nothing but the scarlet sarong wrap worn on the day the show went Indonesian. She grabbed it. Anything, even an old towel, was better than her current dress, stained as it was with petunia soil, obviously slept-in—and even more obviously recognizable from the day before.

Crouching away from the window, Sophie slithered into the skimpy scrap and managed to find a comb in her desk drawer along with tissue to scrub off the worst of yesterday's makeup. Before she could even begin to track down Agnes, she was spotted. The furor exploded in all directions around her.

Now it was almost six-thirty. Sophie still wore the sarong as she escaped out the side entrance. Luckily, Allen Gardens was within walking distance, for Sophie had neither access to her car nor money for a cab. But why, she wondered, did he have to choose a botanical gardens open to the public all day long?

Once inside the fanciful Victorian glass domes, she realized that of all the possible places nearby, this was the one where they were least likely to be seen. Lush tropical plants obscured every inch of the winding paths. It was almost as good as meeting in the depths of the Congo.

"Here!" husked a voice behind her. Sophie spun to find Claude leaning against white ornamental ironwork. Fans of palm made a dense green background. Huge, dusky purple blossoms hung from a vine that climbed beside him high up into the dome in a mass of glossy leaves. Late afternoon light bathed him in a shifting, dappled glow, turning his rough cotton chinos and sleeveless tank top into the gilded pelt of some jungle beast. He stood perfectly motionless, looking so indescribably sexy Sophie could only stare, faint with longing, her mind suddenly blank of turmoil, blank of everything save her steamy reaction to the man in front of her.

Sophie's purse sat on a lip of stonework beside Claude. A fountain splashed water down into a mossy pool where pale pink water lilies glimmered and goldfish lazed in the depths below. She didn't even notice it—or that Claude stood, poised for hot speech—speech that had died wordlessly as his gaze caught the draped scarlet of Sophie's sarong and her shoulders, bare and whitely gleaming under the vaulted glass roof. The thick, sensual humidity of the place had turned Sophie's hair into a mass of curling tendrils and added a light sheen of moisture to her skin. Her blue eyes caught up the reflection from the pool even as they sparkled with a spirit all their own.

For a long, long moment, the heat inside the dome seemed to trap the two, holding them suspended in some medium other than air. A powerful sensuality shot between them, a vibrant physical awareness kindled the moment they met, stoked to a hungry fire by the long night in the pantry entwined in each other's arms. Sophie felt an almost irresistible force of nature propelling her toward Claude, a force that cared not a whit for squabbles about television shows and trivialities such as Sophie's careful life plan. An awful possibility gripped her.

Maybe I'm in love with the man! Not just infatuated! Sappily, soggily, totally in love!

Immediately, Sophie broke out in great beads of sweat. All she could think of was Stan smiling so engagingly while he came at her like an asphyxiating cloud bent on snatching up total control of her destiny. She wouldn't, wouldn't be buried alive like that by any man!

Swiftly, she snatched up her purse and jumped back, lest the almost visible force field around Claude grab her and never let her go. Her breath came in little pants as she looked at his folded arms, thinking how recently they had held her, how recently she had been kissed. Was he really pleased inside to add Sophie Moore to his collection?

He's not like that, admonished the inconvenient voice inside her head, and you know it. You're just trying to think up excuses to run away!

Part of her wanted so badly to trust, yet the dappled jungle light of the greenhouse gave Claude a pagan, almost predatory look. Sophie could not find words of his that she could cling to, words to anchor the crazy, careening emotion inside. Instead, she clutched her purse to her chest and gave in to a wave of rage, resistance, and reaction to this upheaval in the midst of her life.

"How can you stand there so casually, looking at me like that, after the day I've had today!" she burst out.

She had no sooner wadded the earth-stained dress she had shed into the bottom drawer of her desk than Martin had come roaring in, his simple, prizefighter's face bull red.

"Did you know Claude Lacomte was out cold in the pantry all night?" he demanded. "Food poisoning, everybody's saying. From something he ate on your show. We're not supposed to even throw out the trash. The health inspectors will be here in an hour!"

"Health inspectors!" Sophie had cried, flabbergasted.

"Yes, health inspectors. If they find anything," Martin said ominously, "CXRT would just love a lawsuit! And if there's a lawsuit, it'll be a toss-up as to who'll be liable— the entire network, or just you!"

No sooner had that bombshell exploded than a swarm of officials from the health department descended, poking into every nook and crevice of Studio E, obviously just dying to get something on "Ambrosia." Sophie was grilled intensely as to what she had cooked, how she had cooked it, how she had stored her food and, basically, if she knew the faintest thing about proper food handling at all. On top of this, they played and replayed the tape of the show, discussing every move, trying not to snicker at the explosion between Sophie and Claude.

Through it all, Sophie seethed with barely suppressed outrage, wishing fervently she could toss the truth in those officious faces. Or, worse still, she feared they would uncover her true lack of knowledge, find dread bacteria, and drag her ignominiously to court anyway. When they marched their samples off to the lab in plastic bags, she had a vision of herself, sued to her knickers, unable even to sell pencils on the street.

"They've closed my kitchen," Sophie cried in indignation and humiliation. "Closed it because of you!"

"My position is that it should have been closed the minute you stepped into it," Claude replied, altogether too equitably, infuriating Sophie still further. She flung up her hands, almost dumping her purse into the goldfish pond.

"How could you do this to me! Do you know that Lola phoned me up just before I left? She wanted to know if I had been trying to poison the competition. She said that that fight we had would have been even more dramatic if I had actually managed to do you in on air!" Then, since, unbelievably, Claude's face was twitching, "Don't you dare laugh at any of this!"

Sharply, Claude sobered.

"Don't forget, I was caught at a disadvantage too, hungover, barely awake, and with about ten seconds to come up with an excuse. Would you rather," he inquired pointedly, "I had told them the truth?"

Mortification swept over Sophie. Claude did not miss her bright change of color. His breath escaped in a long exhalation.

"I see," he said very softly. "That's how it is."

"Yes, that's how it is!" Sophie fired back in a miasma

of defiance and confusion. The awful thought struck her that Claude had come up with the food poisoning excuse deliberately, even after last night, grabbing the opportunity to make her the object of fun and blow "Ambrosia" out of the water. Oh, that would be intolerable!

"And," she added as a final salvo, "you were eating Galaxy Cakes last night—and darned glad to get them!"

She had got to Claude at last. His brows came down and a muscle popped out on his neck. Now that her eyes had adjusted to the light, Sophie saw he was looking as wasted as she.

"That is a dastardly lie," he spat out. "I know we were drinking cooking sherry. But there isn't enough cooking sherry in the world to make me eat a Galaxy Cake. No way!"

"Yeah? Well here are the wrappers to prove it."

Sophie produced the wad of plastic that had been jammed in her purse ever since dawn when she had swiftly picked up what evidence she could from the floor. Claude looked at them as though finally remembering their contents.

"Touché," he said at last. "Perhaps you can make them your specialty at the big celebrity cook-off."

"What celebrity cook-off?"

"The one our bosses made a deal on today. We're a last-minute substitution next week at the Silver charity banquet. Since you've decided to run me through the wringer, Ms. Moore," Claude suddenly traced his finger all along Sophie's jaw, "I might just use the gala to extract my own sweet revenge."

Chapter Twelve

"Can I fake a coma?" Sophie demanded despairingly of Agnes, the banquet just days away. "Can I flee to Paraguay and take up herding llamas? That man is going trash me in front of half the city. What am I going to do?"

Sophie had stormed into Agnes's bedroom, where she found Agnes sorting through boxes which had remained sealed up under her bed from the day they moved in. Agnes fingered an old tennis racket.

"After your last round with Claude, I refuse even to touch that one."

"You have to! You're my only real backup, Aggie. And why this box binge?"

"Grand purge. I'm getting rid of as much as I can."

Agnes's face bore a peculiar expression which pierced Sophie with swift alarm. This kind of housecleaning always meant upheaval and change. Very slowly, Agnes set down the racket.

"I'm resigning from CAM, Sophie. Sid and I are going to get married—and take over his uncle's sheep ranch in B.C."

Sophie sat down hard on the bed, trying to absorb a shock that snatched away even her powers of speech. Agnes rocked back on her heels.

"You don't look very happy for me."

"What? Oh . . . I am, Aggie, honest I am! It's just that it's all so . . . well, you dropped it on me just like a bomb!"

But even as she congratulated Agnes, and congratulated

her convincingly, Sophie did it with a feeling of unreality
that would not leave even as they unearthed the half bottle
of white wine from the bottom of the fridge and drank
toasts out of water tumblers to Agnes's future and sat
amidst the strewn belongings while Agnes spilled the whole
epic tale of Sid's proposal. Sid longed not to report the
weather, but to be out in it, wind and hail, sun and rain.
And Agnes, at last, would get to write her novel. It wasn't
till long after the wine was gone that they got back to
Sophie's problem with Claude.

"Just stand up and take it sportingly," Agnes advised.
"And have a good laugh."

Sophie flopped across the bed.

"I will not! He'll go round smirking about it for the rest
of his life! Or mine! Whichever lasts longer."

"Hey, lighten up! It's only a silly cook-off, not the clash
of Godzilla and the Cosmic Gladiators. Everybody knows
you can't cook to save your neck, so why get in a pother?
The important thing is to lose gracefully."

"Oh yeah! Well haven't I read all those cookbooks?
Haven't I practiced, haven't I taken enough abuse on my
show? I'm not just folding up and giving in because . . ."

"You're getting that bulldog look again. I really don't
think I can take that look much more."

"You won't have to," Sophie cried before she could
stop herself. "You'll be off in the hills with Sid, counting
sheep!"

Taut silence fell between the two women.

"You make it sound like a crime," Agnes said in a
whisper.

Well it is a crime, Sophie wanted to shout. It is a crime
just to go off with some man and leave me hung out to
dry. We were always going to stick together—through
thick and thin! Through unemployment and heartbreak and
dreadful lemon cream pies and . . . ohhhhh . . .

She caught her breath before it turned into a wail. "I'm
sorry," she apologized miserably. "I'm sure you're going

to be very happy." From Agnes's eyes, she knew this was perfectly true.

Almost instantly, she felt Agnes's arm around her, an unusual gesture from her generally humorous roommate.

"When you're in love," Agnes told her, "a rock in the ocean, never mind a sheep farm, looks like heaven if your man is on it. I can't wait to be there with Sid."

Sophie bit her lip harder, to keep it from quivering. She could not, would not, suffer the final humiliation of bursting into maudlin tears of loss. Agnes squeezed her tighter.

"I've got to go with Sid, Sophie. It's time. It'll soon be your time too. Maybe your time is already here, if only you and Claude could . . ."

"Don't mention him!" Sophie exploded, all her turmoil over Agnes exploding into this ready outlet. "He is the most exasperating, self-satisfied, stiff-necked prig in the city, and if I could hop a plane this minute and leave, I would!"

There was, of course, no question of escape. The instant the substitution was publicized, the banquet was sold out. Never in its history had the event hauled in so much cold cash. There were even rumors of the organizing committee scrapping their own guest tickets. Sophie retreated behind a pillow.

"Save the pep talk, Aggie, I'm not falling for it again. Let's face it! I've been replaced in the newsroom, I'm stuck in a show I'll never be any good at, I'm being forced to be the joke for fifteen hundred bug-eyed spectators, and my best friend is running away to a sheep ranch. Everything's just grand!"

And—I'm in love with Claude, she added in wretched silence, admitting the knowledge that had finally forced itself upon her. Once again she was full up with heartache, just as she'd been after Stan. This was what she had been afraid of, been fighting so hard, she thought. Her struggles hadn't made a jot of difference. She had to put in her stint as one of the walking wounded and there wasn't a thing she could do about it.

Agnes began stuffing boxes back under the bed regardless of their contents.

"Sophie, this really is unlike you. I'm not going near any sheep ranch until I get you straightened out again!"

Even wallowing in the deepest, darkest pit of despair, Sophie still suffered from curiosity. Faintly, from under the pillow, she asked, "How?"

"We'll go shopping for the most drop-dead dress on the continent and stick the Buckeroo with the bill!"

On the night of the gala, a limousine transported Sophie to the event. Sophie rode in its luxurious depths, head high, hair upswept into Salon Ronalda's grandest style. Her body was swathed in the dress she and Agnes had finally come upon in a store Sophie assumed only oil sheikhs and Donald Trump dared venture into. Of burgundy watered silk jersey and practically backless, it changed color every time Sophie moved, and was so cunningly draped in dozens of tiny folds that Sophie seemed to actually shimmer as she walked. The pale cream skin of her throat and arms glowed translucent against it. Agnes's expensive perfume embraced her in a fragrant cloud and the heirloom garnets once again lay shot with ruby light. If she were going down, Sophie meant to do it just like the *Titanic*—with the band playing, all flags flying, and the captain facing down fate on the bridge.

Just outside the hotel where the event was to take place, a crowd forced the limousine to a halt. Claude's admirers, Sophie supposed, and she had no intention of being held up if she could help it. Before the driver could object, Sophie hopped out, meaning to find a nice inconspicuous side door.

Foolish hope! The moment her feet hit the pavement, she was spotted. "It's Sophie!" someone cried, and the attention of the crowd pivoted to her like a compass needle to the pole. Sophie braced herself, determined to handle it with class.

Amazingly, instead of gibes, the crowd began to agitate

with pleasure. Shouts of, "Here she is! It's really her!" rose up. Hands reached out, rows of smiling faces turned toward Sophie, who stopped in confusion, wondering how to escape.

"Can I have your autograph?" cried a woman next to her.

"Me too," put in another. "I love your show. It makes me happy for the rest of the day."

Yet another clutched at her elbow. "I used to just die if people came over for dinner and everything wasn't perfect. Now I don't care. They take me as they find me . . ."

"We came to hold up your side. Go get 'em in there!" Sophie suddenly found herself swept up into the crush, nearly jostled off her feet. Then two large hotel security men were at her side, forming a physical bulwark against the human enthusiasm all round. Someone shouted Sophie's name again—and suddenly the entire crowd seemed to be yelling. Waves of sound came at Sophie. Incredulously, her ears began to make sense of the tumult. The crowd was chanting. Chanting her name!

"So-phie! So-phie! So-phie! So-phie!"

The noise swelled and rebounded off the buildings across the street. The security men had to force a path through the crush—and almost had to pick Sophie up physically as the truth burst upon her. These weren't Claude's fans. They were hers!

All women too. Women in sweaters and cloth coats and sweatshirts. Women who could never afford a ticket to the glittering event inside. Nevertheless, they had all showed up to give Sophie their support in the massively publicized head-to-head with Claude Lacomte.

Before she could digest any of this, Sophie was hustled inside the hotel and into the hands of Mrs. Alicia Thorpe, her personal escort. Mrs. Thorpe whisked her to a private salon just behind the hall where the event was to take place. The salon was buzzing with people, none of whom Sophie knew—except for Claude.

He stood halfway across the broadloom from her, splendid as a duke in his evening clothes. For a moment, Sophie saw nothing else in the room but him, her heart bounding to meet him, her breath hitching in the back of her throat.

The instant she looked at him, he seemed to know. He turned from speaking to a wide-eyed, faintly flushed lady and caught Sophie in his leaf-green gaze. In a fraction, he took in every sweeping detail of her dress, the myriad wayward tendrils of hair, the familiar garnets again nestled warmly at her throat. Sophie simply stood there, unable to think of anything but that pulsing artery just above his collar, the proud set of his shoulders, the tang of pine that would surely intoxicate anyone close enough to catch its subtlety.

By an effort of will, Sophie made the rest of the scene come into focus. Naturally, Claude was surrounded by an entourage—women of every age drawn mothlike to the lure of male attraction. In silver lamé, Marianne glimmered at his side, lovely as a sprite conjured wholesale from morning mist.

Sophie didn't care how many women surrounded him in packs and droves. She only cared what he thought of her; whether he could think of her at all. Was the strong core she sensed in him actually real—or had she too fallen for the beguiling illusion? Had she been a challenge, something to be toyed with and caught, then left behind with a smile as Claude waltzed on to his next interest?

A thought too raw for contemplation! When Claude seemed to step toward her, Sophie turned rapidly away, the confusion in her breast making her putty in the hands of Mrs. Thorpe, who chatted nonstop and kept a constant, bejeweled hold on Sophie's arm.

As the time for Sophie's entrance approached, her nerves turned to wreckage. The crowd was to be seated around tables in the great hall while Claude and Sophie, at the front, simultaneously whipped up their chosen specialties. The results were to be immediately auctioned, the highest bidders winning the privilege of dining on the publically produced creations. The amount of money staked for each created meal was going to graphically illustrate who was the winner here.

"It's time," cooed Mrs. Thorpe. "I'm sure you've checked your setup out there."

Sophie hadn't, but she nodded anyway, knowing exactly what the preparations would be. Gripped with a fatalism totally unlike herself, Sophie had left it all to Joel and Beth. Anxious that Sophie make an impression, they had chosen the fanciest efforts from "Ambrosia," swearing that Sophie, with so much more experience, could not possibly blunder this time. They didn't see Sophie lift her head grimly—preparing silently for public execution.

Just at the door, Agnes suddenly burst through, flags of color on her cheeks, eyes dancing with excitement.

"Where have you been!" Sophie cried reproachfully. Agnes had promised to stick with her every step of the way.

Agnes dragged Sophie away from Mrs. Thorpe.

"What is it?" Sophie demanded. She hadn't seen Agnes look like that since the two of them filled the men's showerheads with blue dye back in college.

"The cook-off's going to go great!" Agnes whispered. "I fixed up everything out there. Listen!" Agnes talked swiftly into Sophie's ear.

"You didn't!" Sophie gasped, perfectly rigid now.

"I did! All you do is add water and heat. Not a thing can possibly go wrong."

"But . . . that's cheating!" Sophie gulped at the amount of money the patrons had forked over for this event.

"And it's about time—the things those assistants expected you to do! You're not going to wimp out on me are you?"

"Well . . . I . . ."

Agnes shook Sophie by the shoulders.

"Oh, come on! Where's the sneaky, devious, brazen character I love so well? A woman who knows how to use her wits!"

Too late to stop this, too late to change! Sophie fixed a bravely wooden smile on her face. What Agnes expected her to pull off was going to take the gall of Godzilla and, if the crowd got mad, maybe even the muscle.

"That's my girl!" Agnes applauded. "Claude's going to get a surprise too, but never mind. I've got the most amazing news..." Measuring Sophie's queasy look, Agnes suddenly stopped. "No! You're in no condition. I better not tell you till afterward. If you start getting shaky, I'm right over there in the corner where you can see me."

Mrs. Thorpe swooped in and bore Sophie off in her smiling, beringed clutches. The next thing Sophie knew, she was being marched out under acres of blazing chandeliers to face the jeweled mob already ensconced around dozens of decorated tables. As Claude came out, glittering bosoms heaved and black tuxedos straightened. They look like a pack of Romans at the arena, Sophie thought glumly, ready to eat me alive!

Well, let them try. Sophie straightened too—and whipped the cloth from the items Agnes had so sneakily, and at great risk, supplied. A shocked murmur ran through the crowd. Beth and Joel blanched the color of old cardboard. Agnes flashed a surreptitious thumbs-up sign.

In place of the umpteen finicky ingredients Beth and Joel had planned, there stood only a single box of meal-in-a-minute macaroni with its own packaged cheese sauce. Next to it was beef and broccoli in one of those plastic pouches that needed only to be submerged a minute in boiling water, then served. For dessert, a heap of mini green marshmallows waited along with a can of the neon pink spray-on whip that gave them such festivity. To Sophie and Agnes, these were childhood familiars all. Familiar and foolproof.

Bravely, not daring to look at Claude, Sophie began. To pull off this feat was going take iron nerve indeed. The least sign of weakening, the least uncertainty and she really would have to move to Argentina. If she didn't actually die of embarrassment on the spot, that is.

Spine rigid, Sophie worked as slowly as she could, for a bit of boiling water and a couple squirts of pink whip and she'd be done. Fixed in the eye of the crowd, she'd had no idea time could pass so slowly. As each excruciating second ticked past, she became more and more vividly aware of Claude, just a few feet away, smoothly working his usual magic. His offering was planned as a surprise, the same as hers had been, but she had no doubt it was something complicated, exquisite, and with a name that lilted singingly off the tongue in French.

Sophie made the mistake of glancing sideways. She caught the gleam of silver dishes, the pattern of artichoke hearts, the wink of Waterford crystal cruets holding rare herbed vinegar and aromatic oils. Most of all, there drifted to her the distinct, redolent scent of truffles, fixed forever in her mind from Mallory's. Claude was creating food for kings, while she—oh, she was trying to pass off a dish harassed moms slapped in front of toddlers for lunch on those days when they had neither time nor money for a real meal.

And Claude's mouth! Why was it quirked in? Why were his eyes dancing like that? Was he waiting for her inevitable crash? Was he already laughing uproariously inside?

Suddenly Sophie felt the core of herself crumble. What was the use! Whatever had made her suppose she could actually brazen this out, dare such audacity? She had only managed to make herself into a joke again. She was done, finished, kaput. She might as well flee now before Claude turned his head and looked straight at her. Her hands began to shake. She slopped water over the edge of the pot in which the macaroni was boiling. It hissed on the burner, perilously close to extinguishing the hot blue flame. In a moment she was really going to spill something and . . . and . . .

Out of the corner of her eye, she caught Agnes signaling. Backed against a curtain where only Sophie could see her, Agnes was holding up an unfolded paper napkin. On it, she had hastily scrawled, "Hooper nabbed! Yr. info! Lead tomorrow!"

For a full three seconds, Sophie stood transfixed. Ellis Hooper had been arrested for arson—on clues she herself had provided. And the story was going to be Greer's lead tomorrow on CAM! This must have been the news Agnes had been so excitedly saving. And the one thing she knew would put the spine back in Sophie at this supremely critical moment in the cook-off!

Brace Sophie it did! She had made it as a newsperson. She was validated, she was real. No possible food disaster could touch her now!

With a flourish, she gave the macaroni a stir and turned up the heat on more water to dunk the beef and broccoli pouch in. Neither could be goofed up short of pouring in drain cleaner—and Agnes had prudently not provided that addition. Her meal, she decided, was actually brilliant in its simplicity, its statement on modern urban folkways, its testimony to the genius of food processors everywhere. Why that crowd out there ought to be *proud* to eat it. Who knew how many of them had made their bucks out of peddling the stuff.

"Go get 'em!" the woman outside had urged, and that was just what Sophie meant to do. Meant to because she was finally digesting the meaning of the scene outside the hotel. Those women had been her fans. Sophie really was famous, a celebrity in her own right. Why else did she need two secretaries to deal with her mail! Why else was she being recognized more and more when she went out! Why else was the Buckeroo getting fat from the ad revenue on her show!

She had attracted her audience and she had kept it. And kept it not because she was a lousy cook but because she was good on the air. She, too, had presence, personality, charisma—all those gilded indefinables, sought so desperately by studio executives, that kept people coming back and back for more!

Why, I'm not only good, she realized in a lightning sear of revelation, I'm absolutely terrific at my job!

For the first time, Sophie tasted the true wine of fame—and grew bold enough to turn again to Claude. She half expected him to be bowled over by the pride surely radiating from her breast. But instead, he was frowning unbelievingly down at his work station. Something in the silver chafing dish was turning his lovely venison medallions black!

Sophie couldn't believe it either—until she remembered more of Agnes's breathless words; "Claude is in for a surprise too . . .''

Agnes had been a whiz in Chemistry 101. She must have done a bit of sabotaging on the side!

Everything ground to a halt while chagrined members of the entertainment committee conferred, for in the face of such disaster how could they carry on with the auction? The crowd waited breathlessly, buzzing with consternation, its attention focused relentlessly on Sophie.

They think I did it! she realized, feeling her confidence crumble again. And the charity is going to lose buckets of money because of an adolescent trick!

She knew Agnes hadn't got so far as to think of that aspect of her action. She'd only been trying protect her roommate. Oh, no matter how many sheep farms she retreated to, she'd always remain Sophie's dearest friend.

Everyone was looking at Claude now to see how he was taking his moment of public humiliation, the mighty brought low, the sophisticated fox finally outwitted at his own game. Claude was trying to speak to the committee but Mrs. Waller-Brandon, too flustered to listen, brushed him away and picked up the microphone.

"Ladies and gentlemen, in view of the . . . er, circumstance, we are forced to cancel the . . ."

"Five hundred dollars!" someone from the audience shouted, "for Sophie Moore's dinner!"

"Six hundred!" cried someone else, and the race was on.

Astounded, Sophie could only gape as the bidding war escalated, boosting the sums to astronomical heights. Claude waited until the main combatants at last ran out of steam, then lifted his hand.

"I'll top anyone's bid for Sophie's dinner," he announced, "Provided she marry me into the bargain."

Sophie didn't happen to be looking at Claude when he said this, and after the words came out, she was unable to turn her head. At such moments the brain operates very strangely. All Sophie's senses became preternaturally alert. She saw the sea of faces before her sway with the impact. She saw the Buckeroo's eyebrows shoot toward his hairline and his head jerk round, telegraphing, before he could stop himself, a look straight to Lola Mallow. A look so full of private, alarmed communication that Sophie hooked an indrawn breath.

Why, he's our spy! The one who's been feeding information to Lola all this time! And he thinks he's going to lose me to Claude—along with all the money coming in from my show.

The Buckeroo jerked his head back—too late. By the time his eye caught Sophie's, he knew he had blown his cover and he knew Sophie knew. His jowls quivered despite an attempt to clamp them tight.

All this happened in the same microsecond it took for Claude's words to sink into Sophie's consciousness. Silence dropped over the hall as though some giant hand had switched the volume off. No one moved, no one breathed, as fifteen hundred drop-jawed glitterati gaped at the two figures poised at the front. Even Agnes had sunk like a shot duck into the nearest folding chair.

Marry me . . . marry me . . .

Sophie felt her heart trying to beat but it seemed stuck somewhere at the bottom of her chest. She lifted her head, willing herself to meet Claude's eyes, quaking at what she might read there.

"C . . . Claude," she got out, "if this is some new kind of . . . of joke, I'll boil you in oil myself!"

"Oh, it's no joke." Claude remembered to reach for the off switch of the microphone they were both hooked up to, throwing them into a tiny circle of privacy. "I mean every word."

He actually looked as though he did. All the teasing roguishness was wiped from his face. The skin over his cheekbones was taut with some inner tension and his eyes were so blazingly green Sophie wondered why she had never appreciated the force in him before.

"I . . . didn't think you were the marrying kind." The words bumped against each other, as Sophie had trouble talking straight. And she felt she had to find objections, arguments, anything while the inmost part of her tried to deal with the cataclysm.

"I could say the same of you. You've spent a lot of energy giving that impression. However," a lean cheek quivered with a half-born smile, "I'm gambling my heart that it's otherwise."

Gambling his heart!

Could it be? Could it be that Claude truly loved her? Desperately, Sophie searched his face and found only unwavering intent.

"You never told me any of this before," she got out weakly, knowing that she sounded quite inane.

Claude advanced a step.

"Have you any idea how hard it is to tell you anything, Sophie Moore?" The familiar flush touched his face. "Or just how dangerous you are to be near? That's when I first fell in love with you, you know, though I didn't guess it at the time—it was just before that fire hose hit us. I saw you dragging me through those fire lines and I thought, now there's a woman a man could take up with and never again be bored. You're the spice of life, Sophie dear. Hot like pepper, wild as Madras curry. Once a fellow tastes it, he's hooked for life."

Even just standing there, he could mesmerize a girl.

"What about all those . . . women on your show?" Sophie demanded, not sure she liked the tenor of a speech about hot pepper.

"What about them!" he returned, and from the dark flare in his eye, she knew, as she had known all along, that her question was unworthy. When Claude made his decision, he gave himself—once and for always. A decision he had never made before. One he was wooing Sophie to accept now.

Sophie grew weak all over again at the very idea. Inside her, everything was clamoring passionately, shouting that she loved him, had loved him for ages, demanding why she didn't just step over and take her heart's desire. A vast tide seemed to be rushing through her, sweeping her inevitably toward Claude. She loved him and she wanted him and the sheer strength of her wanting struck fear and made her fight the forces inside herself. Remembering Stan, she suffered a momentary choking sensation.

"A girl can't just snap up a . . . a marriage proposal just like that!" she protested distractedly.

Heat and cold raced over Sophie at the same time, and the chandeliers were beginning to reel. She felt inundated with longing—and petrified with terror about surrendering to the overpowering pull. Claude read her fear and lifted his palms in a small, disarming gesture of support.

"Why not? If it's conscience that's bothering you, don't forget I have blatant self-interest in mind. I want to be married to the best newswoman in Toronto."

He was trying to tell her that he would always support her, that he would never try to wrest away her destiny, as Stan had tried to.

She had to believe him! She had to trust him!

Her gaze sought his, and suddenly there was nothing else in the room but this entrancing man. She saw behind his smile how terribly vulnerable he had made himself for her, what an awful risk he had taken, speaking up as he had.

"Besides," he added, coming another step closer and taking her hand, "I'm giving up my career as a sex object. Remember that institute we talked about? I've decided to set it up—and I could use a partner with one or two bright ideas."

"I should hope," Sophie got out between dry lips, "you won't completely give up being a sex object. At least for me."

Her heart had got free now and was beating like a kettledrum. Claude's eyes burned with a green, smoky fire that said more than a volume of declarations. Vibrating with gladness, Sophie could no longer remember what any of her objections were. Claude slowly lifted her hand to his lips.

"We'll spring you from 'Ambrosia' as soon as we can."

"Oh, never mind that. I've already got a plan. 'Ambrosia' will go weekly again. I'm going to hold the Buckeroo up for my own public affairs show."

This intention had blossomed, fully formed, in Sophie's mind the moment Claude's lips had touched her skin. He paused in surprise.

"How?"

A ghostly grin touched Sophie's mouth. "Oh, I've got something on him now. I'll make him an offer he can't refuse."

Blackmail about Lola shouldn't be necessary. The Buckeroo simply couldn't afford to lose her—or her drawing power. She admired the old pirate for staying stubbornly afloat so long in such shark-infested waters. He and Lola had been a team for years, keeping each other going—the same as she could be a team with Claude.

His mouth found her palm now and the whole universe began to reel. Sophie swallowed, not caring how much tell-tale blood was rushing to her cheeks.

"Who . . . who's going to do the cooking?" she asked.

"Let's save marital discord until after the honeymoon."

He was up to her elbow again, just the way he had been in Mallory's. This time Sophie was hearing his every word.

And he said, "You still haven't given me your answer."

Sophie had stopped fighting now, couldn't remember why she had even put up a struggle. Her heart flowed out to Claude in a swift, unstoppable river of emotion.

"I think," she whispered, in perfect gladness, "there's definitely a spot open in daytime."

The next thing she knew, she was in Claude's arms and everyone in the hall was madly applauding. His kiss shot straight through her, transporting her to unimagined realms of bliss even while the roar from the spectators shook the crystal on the tables and matched the thump of Sophie's heart.

After an interminable time, a time in paradise, Claude lifted his head away and looked at her, his look struck through and through with joy. The room came back into focus, along with the scent of scorching from the burner Claude had quite forgotten to turn off. He planted himself firmly on Sophie's side of the room.

"And to further prove my love," he laughed, "I'm even going to eat that dessert of yours. We don't dare waste the most expensive green marshmallows in the history of the world!"